PROBABILITIES

By the same author

PORTRAIT OF A YEAR: A MEMOIR

WHAT'S FOR BREAKFAST

THE BEAUTIFUL ART OF ENAMELLING

AN AUSTRALIAN WILDFLOWER DIARY

MY WILDFLOWER JOURNEYS

PROBABILITIES

SHORT STORIES

by

NINETTE DUTTON

All characters in this book are entirely fictitious, and no reference is intended to any living person.

Publication assisted by the Literature Board of the Australia Council, the Federal Government's arts funding and advisory body.

ANGUS & ROBERTSON PUBLISHERS

Unit 4, Eden Park, 31 Waterloo Road, North Ryde, NSW, Australia 2113, and 16 Golden Square, London W1R 4BN, United Kingdom

First published in Australia by Angus & Robertson Publishers in 1987
First published in the United Kingdom by Angus & Robertson (UK) Ltd in 1987

National Library of Australia Cataloguing-in-publication data.

Dutton, Ninette, 1923-
Probabilities.

ISBN 0 207 15375 2.

I. Title.

A823'.3

Typeset in 11pt English Times
Printed in Singapore

CONTENTS

A WELL-CONTENTED MAN

A blackbird bounced across the lawn, poking its beak into the grass every few yards, searching for grubs.

"Chuck, chuck, chuck," it called. Then it sprang onto a low branch and burst into passionate song, its farewell to the fading day.

The late afternoon sun thrust a slender beam through a chink in the drawn curtains and laid it across the face of the girl lying on the bed, her dark hair falling thickly over the pillow. She opened her eyes and looked into those of the man lying beside her. He lifted his hand and pushed back a cascade of hair from her forehead. It was so richly luxuriant that it was sometimes in the way of their lovemaking, and though she would pin it back as she stepped naked towards the bed, it always came tumbling down. He ran his hand over the slope of her shoulder.

"The most beautiful back I ever saw."

She laughed at him in her throat and with her fingers described a circle round his buttocks.

"The most beautiful bum," she said.

He slapped her lightly where the sun had left a small white bikini on her brown bottom.

"Disrespectful girl." He stretched an arm across her. "I must go now, you know."

"What time does your plane leave?"

"At eleven I leave, but there's a family party at home before and I promised I'd be early. The children are coming and bringing their kids."

He kissed her eyelids. "I can't bear to leave you."

"Go," she said. "Quickly."

When she heard him in the shower, she curved a languorous arm under the bed and pulled out a tape-recorder whose spool was slowly turning.

"Kiss. Kiss. Kisses. Goodbye, my love," she said softly into the machine and, switching it off, removed the tape. She took a pen from the bedside table and, after considering a suitable title, wrote on it, "Night and Day".

He had once told her it was his favourite song.

> In the roaring traffic's boom
> In the silence of my lonely room
> I think of you...

She put the cassette in a plain business envelope and wrapped a gown around herself.

While he was lacing his shoes, he heard her moving about in the kitchen, busy with small tasks there, turning on a tap, putting down a plate. Though it had been some off-beat quality of hers, an unusual kind of beauty which had drawn him to her, he loved too the domestic side of her nature, the competent way she handled household objects, made her rooms comfortable, set food upon the table. She was humming as she moved about, a haunting little folk tune, and she repeated the refrain over and over again. Her lively good spirits were part of her attraction for him. She never grumbled or complained.

"No scenes," she had said very early in their relationship and there never had been. He disliked scenes and avoided them at all costs. "Emotional extravagance," he called them, and he did not care for any form of waste.

He usually walked home when he left her. It was not a great distance and it gave him an opportunity to adjust his thoughts, a bridging time. Besides, he felt so vigorously alive when he left her that he could almost have run the whole way.

Since a driver called for him in the mornings to take him to the city, and he sometimes had the man leave him at a nearby park in the afternoons, no one thought anything of his arrival home on foot. Occasionally the girl drove him back to his office in her car, but it seemed an unnecessary risk and in any case, he preferred the intimacy of saying goodbye in the house, a last kiss, eyes locked together as he paused by the gate and she stood at the front door. The pangs of farewell, the anticipation of the next meeting, were all expressed in that look.

Today, as he was leaving, the girl put the envelope in his hand, closing his fingers over it and kissing them as she did so.

"It's a tape I made for you and you're not to play it until you reach London," she said.

"I'd hardly have an opportunity anyway," he replied. "What have you put on it for me, girl?"

"You'll see," and she smiled secretly.

He set out briskly. He knew the street "by heart", he had once said to her, for he had walked along it every day as a little boy going to and from school. He held himself well; his lithe carriage and clipped grey moustache gave him a military air, as though he had once been in the army, but this was not so. He had been a bomber pilot in World War II, and in those days his moustache had flowed long and silky brown over his top lip.

He strode along enjoying the balmy evening and the pleasant melancholy of his thoughts, mixed with agreeable anticipation of the dinner to come with his wife and family. He hummed the little folktune the girl had been singing in the kitchen.

Some of the fences he passed were the same as they had been sixty years before. Fences were so important when you were a child and not tall enough to see over them. There was the stone wall covered with ivy, neatly cut now, but in those days straggling out over the path to catch at his hair and dropping leaves on the pavement. They miraculously turned to brown skeletons in wet midwinter and he collected them and kept them in a drawer in his room. The next fence had once been brown-painted galvanised iron and it had been a forbidden pleasure to run his school ruler along it. Not only did the rattling enchant his ear, but the vibration of the ruler in his hand gave him great satisfaction. The galvanised iron was gone now, replaced by a more fashionable brush fence. After that came cast-iron rails, set in a stone base and protecting a hedge of blue plumbago whose pale slender flowers he used to pick and suck for their honey. He used also to clash his ruler on these rails and they rang a kind of tune. Finally, he came to a brick wall, very high. Even now in his tall manhood, he could not see over the top. Now he turned the corner into another street.

At the end of this street he came to the main road, noisy with late afternoon traffic streaming towards the outer suburbs. Just here stood a phone box. Placing his briefcase on the shelf of the phone box, he opened it and stowed away the girl's gift which he had been carrying under his arm. Suddenly he longed to hear her voice just once more. He was still within what he thought of as her territory. On the far side of the torrent of cars there was a different land; the next tree-shaded street led to the park which adjoined his own house.

He seldom telephoned her but now, fumbling for a coin to put in the slot, he broke his own rule.

"Hullo. This is . . ." and she gave the number. The husky answer was faint and difficult to hear against the traffic noise, but his heart melted within him.

"It's me. I just wanted to say goodbye again and thank you for the tape."

"You nearly missed me. I was going out to get some milk and bread. Thank you for ringing me. Goodbye. Goodbye, my love."

She hung up and left him feeling cold inside and unsatisfied. He wished hc had never touched the wretched phone. She was farther from him now than the mere length of a couple of streets, was going out, shutting the door behind her. Her life without him was starting again.

She would never allow herself to sit about and mope, she had told him so. Despite that, he thought she might have been crying. He had a dread of women in tears and would much rather have thought of her waving as he slammed the gate behind him.

Picking up his briefcase and angry with himself for having been foolish, he pressed the pedestrian button at the traffic lights and crossed the wide road. He had disturbed the peaceful train of his own thoughts, which irritated him, and he now added to his annoyance the realisation that her husband might well have arrived home and answered the telephone. She had told him that he was returning from interstate that evening.

He turned into a street shaded with cedar trees, their little ochre berries beginning to drop on the ground and crack underfoot. He seldom thought about her husband and when he did so it was not with any deep feeling. He had only met him once or twice, before the affair began. The man was away so much of the time, touring the country for his engineering firm, that she was often alone and lonely. Secretly he felt that he was doing the fellow a kindness by keeping his wife happy. It was a justification that he only half admitted, even to himself.

She had described to him her life the first time they met when, unexpectedly, they had found themselves alone in the corner of a garden at a party. There had been a certain awkwardness for a brief space, a lack of something to say, but somehow she had begun talking about herself, and, always a sympathetic listener, he had found himself charmed by her slightly rueful confidences and the provocative way in which she laughed at herself. He longed, at that minute, to take her in his arms, to kiss the place on her bare neck where her heavy hair curved away over her shoulder.

He was startled, shocked. Apart from a few jolly tumbles in his far-off Air Force days, which he considered hardly counted, he had always been faithful to his wife and confidently thought of himself as a good husband. He had not looked for such an extraordinary experience to befall him, something so far removed from the usual orderly scheme of his life. He was a man of habit and kindly good nature, who prided himself on the foresighted plans he made for his family. He had no thought of disturbing these. Yet here in the garden a girl he hardly knew was upsetting all his usual values.

Looking at each other with a surprised half-knowledge, the two turned and walked up the path to the house. When they rejoined the party he went immediately and put his arm around his wife's shoulders, as though for protection.

She smiled and dropped a kiss on his hand. She was a pretty woman, whose looks, relying as much on her expression as on her features, grew upon people the more they came to know her. She was much beloved by a wide circle of devoted friends. Her children not only adored her but exploited her good nature relentlessly, which she thoroughly enjoyed. She was always babysitting or sewing or cooking, to such an extent that her husband sometimes grumbled, though not seriously. In fact he thought these activities suitable occupations for a wife, and she had never made him jealous by neglecting him.

The pavement where he walked had a row of little cracks across it and he automatically stepped over them, as if he were still a child. His mind went back to the girl and he remembered his first days with her, the excitement of their coming together. He had not fought very hard against the unexpected turmoil of feelings which had suddenly burst into his life. It was not in him to resist something which by then he craved, body and soul, and they became lovers at the first opportunity. It seemed that they could hurt nobody and he now considered his life perfectly balanced. He had not realised that it needed an extra dimension, but now he felt that he had everything a man could want. He was well contented. Long before he had known the girl, he had had a favourite aphorism which he brought out from time to time.

He liked to say, "A man needs three women in his life: a wife, a mistress and a secretary. But of course that need only mean two."

"Well, I won't be your secretary," his wife would reply sweetly. "Perhaps I can be your mistress."

"What would you do if I took a beautiful red-headed mistress?" he asked her once.

"I expect I'd take an overdose," she replied and continued to read the evening newspaper.

"Nonsense — I can't stand that kind of melodramatic talk." He was cross. People he knew never killed themselves; his friends did not go in for that sort of thing. He went outside to change the hoses, annoyed that she had darkened his mood in what he had intended as a fancifully flirtatious exchange. He was still aggravated when he came back into the house.

"Those children tire you out," he said pettishly. "They never leave you any time to yourself."

This was not true. She guarded her own time more carefully than he realised. She was an efficient manager and, to her husband's constant amazement, had a remarkable head for facts and figures, something which was uncommon amongst the women he knew. Following the stockmarket was as much a relaxation for her as her weekly game of tennis. He admired the way she ran the household and he knew he could rely on her to arrange a difficult dinner party at short notice, knew that a cold-eyed Englishman with charming manners and the soul of a computer would return to his hotel delighted with himself as a result of her excellent cooking and friendly Australian flattery.

When she sat at their attractive dinner table, well dressed but not ostentatiously so, the candlelight enhancing the corn colour of her fine hair which scarcely showed grey, he could feel confident that the important Chinese businessman from Singapore sitting next to her would be impressed with her grasp of the international market situation and would go home with their name on his lips. Silent Indian wives or high-powered intellectual American ladies did not faze her in the least. She found something to interest her in each of them and enjoyed their company.

He wished nothing to disrupt this smooth-running life in which each activity had its rightful place and its appropriate time. This was well understood, not only by his family, but by his friends and business acquaintances. He appreciated the same imperatives in their lives.

He was not insensible that there were deep currents flowing beneath this smooth surface, but he thought it dangerous to explore their reaches. They were best left alone. He recognised that there were certain qualities about his wife that he had never fathomed. All those books she read, for instance. She was always coming home from the library with something new. He himself made no time for reading books. It was all he could do to finish reading the weekly papers and magazines and watch his favourite television programmes. Occasionally she brought him a biography or a book of memoirs which he enjoyed, particularly if it was about royal or illustrious persons born around the turn of the century.

She went to concerts in the winter, too. He tended to nod off at concerts, so he stayed at home and played the hi-fi. He was particularly fond of the tunes from the musicals of the '50s and sang them well in a fine baritone voice. He did not at all understand the music his children liked and frequently compared notes on the matter with his friends. He was much attached to his children and took a detailed interest in their affairs.

"We have a very good relationship, apart from that loud music," he often said.

He was proud that the three of them, all boys, had university degrees and good jobs. He maintained that this indicated a great deal more good management than good luck and privately took some credit for having brought them up to be sufficiently forceful to succeed in a difficult world.

"I feel sorry, very sorry, for those boys who can't find jobs. Jobs are there, but they won't come to you. You've got to go out and get them," he would say.

He had nearly reached the park now, gazing over the fences at the gardens as he went along. He noticed a bed of Peace roses which were coming into their second flowering; already the dead heads wanted cutting back. Further along a stand of dahlias badly needed staking. He knew that the occupants of the house were overseas. Obviously the garden was being neglected in their absence. He was pleased to see that at number 25 an overgrown blue solanum had been grubbed out and a frangipanni put in its place.

At the entrance to the park he was joined by two friends. The three men often shared this walk home and exchanged the day's news.

At home in their own garden his wife was picking a bunch of little pink Cecile Brunner roses and white daisies for the dinner table. She carried them inside, arranged them in a silver vase and took out a box of pink candles. The room looked festive; it would give her husband a happy memory to carry overseas with him. She wished now that she was going too. She was perfectly capable of running the household and managing their affairs without him, but she missed his company and felt lost when she could not bestow on him all the little attentions he enjoyed so much. Every time he left her to go on a journey she felt as though a piece of herself was being torn away, though she knew that people of her age were supposed to have outgrown such turbulent emotions. He had asked her to accompany him, but the trip was to be so short that it had seemed extravagant. She was always pulled between her own inclinations, her duty towards the children and her duty towards her husband. This time she had refused him, but decided that she could certainly go on the next trip with a clear conscience. She was sorry now that she had not accepted. If it had been possible at the last moment to arrange all the formalities, she would have booked a seat on the plane that very afternoon. But no one made sudden decisions like that to fly overseas. It was too late now.

She put out a plate of his favourite olives and thought affectionately about him. In her view he was the ideal husband. She knew his limitations, but considered them lovable foibles rather than shortcomings. The strengths which were the counterparts of his weaknesses were the rocks upon which she had built her life, and it had been a satisfying one. He had been everything she wanted as a husband and a father. Her own father had been less than perfect as a husband and, such is the strength of childhood experience, she knew by the time she was eighteen that she could never endure the kind of life her mother accepted. She had a clear idea of the man she wanted and, surrounded by eager wartime suitors as she was, she waited a long time to find the fulfilment of her ideal. When he appeared, she knew at once that he was the one; soon they were inseparable and before long they were married. Since then there had been no other man for her. While she only half-believed in formal promises, her life was so completely fulfilled that she had never contemplated breaking those she had made on her wedding day. She often thought she had been happier than most. Sometimes, waking in the desolate hours before dawn, she wondered superstitiously if she had not been too happy, if all her life's troubles still lay ahead of her.

She liked to look back on the years since her marriage. It was an endless entertainment to look at the photograph albums which she kept assiduously up to date. Such was her nature that she hardly remembered the bad moments but dwelt on the good times in detail. Of course there had been frights and distresses of various kinds. There was the time when one of the boys had a bad fall from his bike, and another when an appendix threatened to burst before an operation could be performed. There were triumphs and failures in examinations and sports and with girlfriends. One of the boys was slightly dyslexic and had had difficulty writing essays. She taught herself to type so that she could make notes for him. Nowadays she occasionally used her skill to help her husband. When he had something extremely confidential he sometimes brought it to her instead of entrusting it even to his excellent secretary.

"If I turn into your secretary, I hope I don't stop being your mistress," she teased him, but he kissed her cheek rather perfunctorily and turned away as if to change the subject.

Then, perhaps feeling he had been noticeably ungallant, he said, "I'd like all my secretaries to be as pretty as you."

All the joys and despairs of family life had been brought to her and she had dealt with them and shared them with her husband when she considered it wise. Sometimes she wondered if she were not merely a filter instead of a positive force in the family, but that was not so. It was she who set the tone at home.

As her husband understood that there was a side of her life that was beyond his grasp, so she knew that there was a part of his experience that was different and aside from her own. Through his work he met a curious mixture of people and found most of them fascinating. Because they were not a part of his social scene, they were suitably distanced from him and he could allow himself to enjoy their strange manners and extraordinary stories and to respond to them in a way he could never do with his family friends. He had at times to deal with truckies and kangaroo shooters, stonemasons and bookbinders.

Her sophistication came from the eclectic range of books which she read constantly in order to find out more about the world beyond her own immediate circle. His was of a different kind, derived from direct contact with people. They complemented each other and respected each other's separate world.

She put down a pile of clean clothes on the bed, ready to pack for him. He was not good at such things and preferred her to do it. Everyone would be here for dinner at any minute.

As they crossed the park the three friends chatted amicably. They remembered well the days when the park area was only rough grass with a few grazing cows and horses and fat cowpats to trap unwary feet. Now the grass had been cut and the earth chopped into flowerbeds, rectangles and lozenges, filled at present with gaudy cannas, red and yellow and strident pink. Between the beds the council gardeners had planted hybrid bottlebrush, whose weeping leaves softened the military precision of the ferocious army of flowers. The men parted at the end of the path, from where he could see his front gate. His children and grandchildren were just arriving.

"Grandpa, come and play French cricket. I've got a new bat." They clamoured around him. Over their heads he caught his wife's eye as she came to greet the excited group. He slipped his arm around her waist and kissed her cheek.

"Only ten minutes, then." She laughed and hugged them all. "I've got champagne cold and Grandpa must see whether I've packed all he needs."

Everyone talked at once all through dinner, the young children exuberant at being included in the grown-up party, their parents full of a project to buy a piece of land near the sea, about which they wanted to consult their father before he left. When the last helpings of passionfruit flummery, of strawberries and raspberries from the garden were finished and no one could manage another bite, the woman said firmly, just as she had said hundreds of times before:

"Now then, everybody, it's time you went home. It's late for the little ones. No, I'm taking Grandpa to the plane myself and he hasn't finished packing. No, thank you, I can manage beautifully. I'll ring you all tomorrow."

Noisily they crowded down the path.

"Say thank you for having me."

"Say have a good trip, Grandpa."

They were gone and she stood silently with him in the moonlight. She needed this interval of quiet alone with him before they parted. He was humming a little tune as they stood there.

"What's that tune?" she asked.

"Oh." He sounded startled. "Just something I heard this afternoon," and he walked inside.

In the bedroom she turned to practical details to prevent this last half-hour becoming unbearably tense for her.

"Six sports shirts. That should be enough. I put medicines in that blue bag. I got those sleeping pills you wanted — they're in the kitchen."

"Good." He was pleased. "I should be able to get at least a few hours sleep on the plane."

"Handkerchiefs in that corner. We'd better go when you're ready."

Conversation on the way to the airport had a forced cheerfulness. Both were anxious to embark on the dreariness of the next few hours so that they might the sooner be left behind.

His flight was due to be called shortly. As he was about to embrace her he exclaimed suddenly:

"I nearly forgot. I've got a tape here I'd like you to type for me. It's most important. Send it express to me as soon as possible. I dictated it in the office last thing this afternoon."

From his briefcase he drew out a plain envelope and handed it to her. Such was his agitation that he hardly remembered to kiss her at all and hurried towards the gate as she gave a last gesture of farewell.

She drove home carefully, her mind sufficiently absorbed with the late traffic to allow her thoughts to follow him only spasmodically as she pictured the plane taking off on the first long leg of its journey and him settling into his seat and ordering a drink.

After he did those things, he decided to work on some papers before he fell asleep. Opening his briefcase, he took them out and then saw the envelope, with the tape that he had dictated that afternoon, tucked into one of its silk pockets. Puzzled, he pulled it out. He knew very well he had just handed it to his wife.

Realisation came to him as he took the cassette from its envelope.

At home loneliness waited in the empty house for his wife. She went to the kitchen to pour herself a drink. Suddenly she noticed his sleeping pills, forgotten, still standing on a shelf. She was almost relieved; she mistrusted such things and seldom took pills herself. She picked up the bottle. Perhaps, as she was so wide awake now, it would be sensible after all to take one herself tonight. She knew she would not be able to sleep for some time. Then she changed her mind. She had a better idea.

"I think I'll start his typing. I might be able to send it off tomorrow and it'll be in London nearly as soon as he is," she said to herself.

Setting up her typewriter and placing the cassette in the tape-recorder, she sat down at the table and pressed the play button.

A DAY TO REMEMBER

Two small boys sat quietly on a bench in the dentist's waiting room. They each had open on their knees a book about Asterix the Gaul, placed there by a kindly intentioned receptionist. Since they both knew by heart nearly every word written about Asterix and sometimes recited passages in unison for their own amusement, they accepted her offering politely, opened the books and sat gazing into space. The receptionist thought that they were nervous and felt sorry for them. Fancy their mother letting two such little boys come here without her.

She was mistaken in her sympathy. As neither of them had ever had anything wrong with his teeth, their regular visits were merely a formality. They liked the dentist — a bluff, cheerful man, he remembered his own youthful days of dread and always took his younger patients early, before school. They particularly admired his remarkable collection of power tools. They were also grateful to their mother for giving them the freedom of the city. Some boys at school had to have someone older with them wherever they went.

Giles, the elder boy, was ten, two years older than his brother Tom. Ten was an important age, a decade. So that Tom should not feel left behind, he had said to him kindly on his birthday:

"You'll soon be a decade."

Tom did not understand, and replied grumpily: "I can't be a decade. That's not what I am."

Giles had to explain, which was surprising. It was not often that he knew more words than Tom who got As for everything at school, whereas Giles sometimes got even as low as a C.

Almost as alike as identical twins, despite the difference in age, both had heavy fair hair, pale as summer grass, which hung down over striking black eyebrows and sheltered their dark eyes. They were inseparable friends, but it was Tom who was always the captain in their enterprises. The boy was a problem to his elders. It was not that he was naughty in an ordinary way. All his misdemeanours resulted in high adventure of an original kind, which nobody had thought to forbid until too late. Giles followed him, generally protesting, but he could never think of better ideas than the ones Tom came up with and, as he had a strong protective feeling towards his younger brother, he felt obliged to keep an eye on him.

Just now they were enjoying the importance of the occasion and the break from their usual routine of catching the school bus. But there was another aspect of this morning which made it different from any other. They both had a great deal of money in their pockets, more than they had ever had to spend in their lives. When their father had left them at the door of the big city building where the dentist had his surgery, he had given each of them a twenty-dollar note, something he had never done before. It had been a strange morning altogether, Giles thought, and as he sat there a cold prickle of goose flesh ran up his spine.

He had been the first one in the kitchen that morning, which was unusual. His mother was generally making their school lunches when he came in, carefully wrapping the cheese or raisins he usually swapped at school for the butterfly cakes with which a friend's mother filled out his lunch box. In the silent kitchen Giles piled a bowl with Weet-bix, yoghurt and bananas and turned on the radio so that he could listen to the news which was required for his Current Affairs class, later in the day. It was very dull; he hated Current Affairs. "Strikes at Whyalla. Light aircraft lost off the coast." It was always the same stuff.

His father strode into the room and roughly turned the radio off.

"I won't have that noise at breakfast. You can't hear yourself think," he barked.

"But, Dad —" Giles was about to protest, but something in his father's face kept him silent.

His mother appeared, still in her dressing-gown, which was not her habit. Giles was unhappy. He liked everything to be seemly and in the customary order. She looked so pretty in the jeans and bright coloured shirts she usually wore in the morning. Now she rushed out of the room, as though she was going to be sick. Giles felt a shiver of unexpected dread; his breakfast was distasteful and he pushed his plate away. There was something wrong with the morning and even Tom crept in silently.

Their mother returned. "You'll have to buy your school lunches today. Your father will give you the money." It was so solemn.

"But, Mum, aren't you going to drive us to the dentist?" asked Giles.

"Oh, God, I forgot the dentist. Well, your father will just have to take you."

"Yes, dear," Dad replied meekly. Again this was surprising. Dad did not like driving them anywhere. Only a few days ago Giles had heard him say to Mum:

"You can't expect me to be running them all over the place. What do you think I gave you that car for?"

Which was a sensible question. He had given her a beautiful cream Alfetta for her birthday and it was a pity to waste it. Dad seldom came to school occasions, except perhaps to important football or cricket matches, but never to speech days, even if one of them got a prize. Looking at the fathers seated in the school hall one prize-giving, Giles had asked:

"Why doesn't Dad ever come?"

"He's much too busy," his mother said tartly. "He has to work very hard to send you to a school like St George's."

Giles understood. He was proud of his school, though not particularly grateful to his father for his exertions — they were something that was expected of a father. He was glad that Dad measured up to a high standard, but Mum was the one with whom they shared their experiences.

Now she said, "You'd better go." But she was not looking at the boys, only at Dad, and she had a white face.

"Do you boys know where to catch the bus to school?"

"Yes, Mum."

"Giles, don't let Tom go off on his own for a moment."

"No, Mum."

She hurried out of the room without even kissing Dad goodbye.

When they were climbing into the car, Dad put a grip-bag into the boot.

"What's that for?" Tom asked inquisitively.

"Oh. That. Oh. Well, I might go jogging this afternoon."

"I didn't know you went jogging."

"It might be good for me," and not another word did he utter until they reached the city, where he actually got out of the car and put his hands on their shoulders. That was when he gave them the money, thrust it at them almost, without seeming to notice that it was much more than they had every had.

It was extraordinary and they could hardly wait to be finished with the dentist and out in the street where they could discuss this phenomenon. Whatever conversation they might have had was too private for this public place, whose hush was made more oppressive by the sound of musak. So the two of them sat side by side in pleasant anticipation.

The dentist was running late and Tom grew bored. He picked up the morning paper and turned the pages, a paragraph here and there catching his eye.

At last the receptionist beckoned them.

After their inspection and an agreeable chat they were free in the sunny street at last.

"What are you going to buy with your money?" Giles was bursting with curiosity.

"Nothing," said Tom. "We're going to Port William."

"Port William, that's eighty kilometres away, I heard Dad say the other day. His boat's there somewhere. How would we get there?"

"By train. It had in the paper about an excursion. We've just got time — the station's only a little way."

"But what about school?"

"They won't know. We've got a letter for this morning, and this afternoon it's the swimming sports, remember. You've got your bad ear and Grade IV's only in the wading race — I'm not going in *that*."

"What about Mum?"

"She won't notice, she couldn't come."

"But we'll be late home."

"Not *very* late." Tom hesitated slightly, but carried on quickly. "There's a special train. Hurry up or we'll miss it."

Tom was clearly determined on the plan and Giles remembered his mother telling him not to let his brother go off on his own. He was persuaded. It was hard to stand virtuously firm against such a beguiling prospect.

"All right, let's go."

At the ticket office on the station concourse Tom hopped from one leg to another, as he always did when he was excited.

"Stop jigging," said Giles sternly, as he had heard his mother do. He had to retain some shred of authority. Tom hardly heard him as he passed over the money for the tickets.

"What are you boys doing?" the man behind the grille asked suspiciously. "Shouldn't you be at school?"

"There's swimming sports," Tom replied glibly, adding under his breath "this afternoon", and keeping his fingers crossed in his pocket. Giles was speechless with guilt.

Neither of them had been on a train before and there was no time to feel guilty in the excitement of it; the way you could move about from side to side and look out all the windows, the thrill of the tunnels. Giles sent one last thought to his mother, a farewell, and gave himself up to the glory of it all.

After they had left that morning, their mother stood in the hall of the house, the heart of her domain, her arms clutched fiercely about her as though her body might fall to pieces and her secret inner self fly away and disappear forever. She was a dark, compact young woman, whose descent from wild Welsh hillsmen showed in her unusual looks. She and her husband had quarrelled bitterly the night before, flagellating each other with their tongues and leaving wounds which she thought might never heal. Now she was exhausted, drained by the evil torrent of words that had poured from her, aching from the vomiting which had come after them and worn out from lack of sleep.

Their quarrels had begun even before they were married. They were a ritual in which each recognised the other's part precisely and knew exactly the bounds beyond which lay destruction. It was she who had started them, teasing and taunting him mercilessly, as though challenging his manhood to force her to declare her love for him and be kind. After their marriage their quarrels acted as an aphrodisiac and, when they came together in the ultimate and expected reconciliation, they always made love more passionately than they did on an ordinary night when he reached out and sleepily rolled her towards him. Their quarrels were secret, darkly hidden. They would no more have quarrelled in public than have made love before an audience, and their friends thought of them as an ideal couple.

To her he was a manly man, all she had ever expected of a

husband. Both the boys were the result of their quarrels, yet she loved them the more keenly because of that and willingly gave her life to caring for them and to making her household a pleasant one. She was an energetic and imaginative mother; their house was charming, with nothing ever out of place. When the boys began school she helped in the school library and was always available to organise trading tables and make costumes for the school plays. As they grew older and their interests took them away from home more often, she found she needed a greater outlet for her energies and took part time work in a public relations firm, where she proved most successful.

It was after she began work that the quarrels grew more serious, more frequent, and less controllable. They were no longer rituals, but bitter fights in which each sought to attack the other as savagely as possible. Proud of her newly earned money, she began bringing home little treats for the family, but her husband carped and complained so much about extravagance, spoiling everyone's pleasure, that she quickly gave up doing so. For the first time she learnt to hide things from him. He felt his place at the head of the family endangered by even the small amount of power that the money gave her. He had always believed that you had to pay for what you wanted, even friendship, and, having paid for it, that you were entitled to certain rights. Somehow, she seemed to be taking these away from him.

Their friends did not guess that there was anything wrong. The quarrels were still secret. If he was particularly demanding or critical when they gave a dinner party, she probably needed it. He knew how to handle women. Good looking in a fair, vulnerable way, he was popular. A yachtsman, he sailed his own boat to win races in the summer, played a good game of golf in the winter, was generous with his wine and knowledgeable about vintages. He had a habit of drawing attention to his faults and mocking them, which was rather endearing. A competitive and ambitious man, he always needed to prove himself, and his friends respected him for that. He thought of his children as appurtenances to the good life, for whom he had a duty to provide, rather than as people with whom he might share his thoughts and pleasures.

The young wife had automatically granted him his place as head of the household, but lately she had begun to find new strengths within herself which she had never suspected lay there and which were not dependent upon him. She had always been glad of her masculine world, seeing herself occupying a privileged place because of it, and had never wanted another child. Now, standing shivering and alone, she suddenly longed for a daughter, a girl who would understand her feelings and her femininity, to whom she could talk without reserve. And now it was too late.

Last night she had told her husband he must leave her, that she no longer wanted him, that their quarrels had brought them at last to the point of destruction. In his anger he had declared that this was all he desired, that he would not spend one more night in the same house as her, that he had only stayed as long as he had because the boys needed a father. They went on and on until they were too tired for more and eventually fell asleep, cold and hard on either side of the bed.

Now she stirred herself and looked around, realising drearily that there were beds to make and dishes to be washed. At that moment she truly hated him for leaving her with this mess, for being free to escape so easily into another world. Probably at that moment his secretary was bringing him a fresh cup of coffee.

His secretary was doing exactly that. She had sensed his mood immediately and suspected something of the cause. A coolly efficient young woman, she had been with him for some years and knew very well how much she had contributed to his rise in the firm. She was fond of him in a tolerant way and was always nice to his wife. She prepared the coffee and placed the cup and saucer on a tray, an attention he appreciated. He disliked sloppy mugs being handed round the office. She placed the mail on the desk beside the tray.

On top lay a long envelope in unusual cream paper. Still cherishing his anger and resentment he found it hard to concentrate on work and absent-mindedly tore the envelope open as he nibbled a biscuit. Then his hand shot out in a gesture of excitement which almost tipped over his cup. The letter was from the New York branch of his firm, and he quickly skimmed the words.

"We are delighted . . . take charge of our office in New York . . . three months time . . . subject to this being agreeable to your wife." And so on. He read it again more slowly. This was the fulfilment of his highest ambition, something he had not really dared to hope would come about. He sat back in his chair to savour the moment better. He could picture already the pleasures and possibilities of such an advancement; the responsibilities did not worry him just now. This would show his wife what sort of man he was. He could not wait to tell her. He could see her eyes light up with admiration. And then he remembered. She had ordered him out of her life, and he had told her that he never wanted to see her again.

Now came this offer. The post was only open to a married man. It was one of the qualifications. There was a great deal of entertaining to be done and important visitors to be looked after. A wife was essential.

They had both joked knowingly together about the tests which had been set for her, yet each had been as eager as the other for her to succeed in them. There had been a lunch in the boardroom with wives and smoked salmon, and she had received a great deal of attention. A few days later there had been a more intimate little drinks party. Finally, he had been asked, tactfully, to entertain one of the American directors and his wife to dinner at his house. This had been the most successful occasion of all. His wife had won them completely with her good cooking, her guilelessly forthright manner and her businesslike knowledge of public relations. He had been pleased with the boys that night too.

"My sons," he said proudly, standing with an arm around each of them, while they courteously said "How do you do?" and shook hands.

The director's wife was enchanted.

"Aren't they just edible!" she cried. "They've both got the same little noses."

She did not know that the boys would spend the next week lampooning herself and her husband. Giles was a good actor and reproduced the American director's benign condescension magnificently; Tom, a true mimic, imitated the lady's cooing tones so accurately that they both rolled on the floor with laughter. Nor did the director's wife notice the small chicken bone placed in the teeth of the chromium jaguar which, mounted on the bonnet, bounded ahead of them down the road as they drove to their hotel. Those candid faces could hide no wickedness; no wonder their parents were so devoted to them. Their mother was a delightful woman and their father obviously most able.

In his office their father managed to attend to his morning appointments, but by midday could face no more. He decided to go off to his boat and spend a night on board; he must sleep somewhere and he did not want to acknowledge his predicament to anyone. His boat had been moored by a friend at Port William, ready for a weekend expedition.

"I think I've got a migraine coming on. I'm feeling terrible," he said to his secretary. "I'm going for a drive — some fresh air might cure it. Deal with anyone who telephones."

He trusted her to cover up for him.

He enjoyed driving and, as he swooped along the freeway and over the hills, his mind began to clear. He hardly knew what he wanted from his marriage now, though he knew very well that he would go to great lengths to be able to take the offered position in New York. Would his wife have him back? Could he bring himself to ask her and, if he did, how would they treat each other? There could be no more quarrels like last night, never again. But perhaps they were so addicted to the drug that they could never break the habit.

He admired his wife for being capable and good humoured and was happy that she was attractive in her foreign-looking way. He would not have wanted her to be a great beauty. He had chosen her and he loved her. When he fought with her it was as if he were fighting something within himself. Perhaps it was that hidden quality which she was fighting also. At this turning point in his life he saw himself with a detachment that he had never known before.

Yet there was something about her which could make him feel inadequate. It was the way in which she accepted the whole of life, not ignoring the bad but favouring the good, as though she had some extra dimension in her nature, some dimension which he could not grasp. He, for instance, was repulsed and irritated by dirty or sick children. She simply tended and washed them and seemed all the better for it, and so she was in many situations which he might have ignored but which she treated with open-hearted cheerfulness. Her immediate recognition of what was needed on these occasions secretly humiliated him. She dealt with situations while he was still considering the means.

He drove on, longing for the comfort that he knew only she could give him, yet unwilling to humiliate himself by asking for it. Sometimes his anger rose uppermost, sometimes more tender feelings. He wondered if she could give him warmth again.

There was also the question of the boys. He had no intention of abdicating his responsibilities.

The boys at present were blissfully content. When the train pulled into the station at Port William, they were sorry that the journey was over but jumped out and followed the other members of the excursion across the gritty station yard. The other members were mostly old people, aged couples helping each other along, a bowling club on its annual outing, and others. Giles and Tom quickly left them behind as they made for the beach. But first came the pleasures of the main street. One fascinating shop window held all kinds of electrical goods, with the very latest gadgets set out in front. They longed for an electric toothbrush. Another displayed gearwheels for various pieces of machinery, all arranged in a pattern. They stayed there for a long time.

Hungry, they bought icecream and chips and then, each with a king-size hamburger-with-everything, they came to the end of the street and into the stinging sun on the foreshore. Here, under the speckled shade of a Norfolk Island pine, they finished their lunch, sitting on the prickly buffalo lawn beside a bed of petunias striped pink and white, like awnings. Tightly replete, they tossed their scraps into a bin made to look like a penguin and dashed for the sand. Quickly taking off their shirts and sandals and hiding them by a rock with their school bags, they raced along the shore, ran as though they could never have enough of running. The little grey dotterels ran ahead of them along the edges of the tiny waves.

Laughing hilariously, they fell gasping on the sand, then, leaping up, began whipping each other with lengths of kelp which lay on the tide-line.

"I'm going to swim," said Tom.

"We haven't any togs."

"There's no difference between jocks and togs. Come on."

They swam and splashed and swam some more.

"Better than the school pool," they shouted to each other.

Waterlogged at last, they wandered along the beach, letting the breeze dry them. They collected shells as they walked back the way they had come towards the jetty which ran out into the curve of the bay, its old grey wooden piles rough with barnacles and shaggy with soft, hair-like weed which floated rhythmically backwards and forwards with the flow of the water.

Giles fetched his shirt from the pile by the rock. "Rub your face with that," he said as he handed it to Tom. Their faces were crisp with caked salt.

On the jetty a few fishermen lackadaisically held rods over the rail. One man, with a bucket full of tommy ruffs beside him, was not talkative and just grunted when they tried to make conversation. Further along the jetty some aged steps led down to the water where a wooden dinghy in need of paint was tied to a post. An old man in a torn grey jersey and with a maroon bobble cap over wispy grey hair was stowing two crayfish pots amidships. He was friendly, and they chatted while he pottered about.

"Going to look at me cray pots and put out two new ones," he said. "You boys want to come?"

"Really?" they gasped simultaneously. This was too much, the high spot of the day.

"If you want to. Don't you want your shirts?"

"I've got one," said Giles, holding up his salty garment.

"I never get cold," said Tom.

"Thought you might get burnt."

"We're burnt already."

Truly, after a long summer, they were toasted as brown as good bread rolls.

Giles helped stow some orange buoys under the thwarts, and the old man handed the oars down to Tom.

"Who's going to be anchorman?"

"I am," said Tom, quickly.

"All right. Go up the bow and you, me boy, can sit in the stern with me next to the outboard. You can steer when we get clear of the jetty."

Tom was a little sorry that he had been so eager to take the first job.

Giles sat happily with one hand on the tiller, adjusting for the wind and the waves. They went on and on until the houses on the shore had shrunk to pink and blue matchboxes. The old man sat silently smoking his pipe, not talking now, directing Giles with a gesture of his arm from time to time. Neither of the boys had expected to come out as far as this and, for a second, Giles felt a twinge of apprehension. What if they missed their train? He put the thought from him. The swell was bigger out here, but the dinghy rode well, up and over, up and over.

The old man straightened.

"I'll take her now. We're getting to the reef."

Waves were breaking ahead and he steered straight towards the white spray. The boys could see no passage through the reef but, just as it seemed that they must be driven onto the rocks, he swung the boat a little and there stretched a narrow lane of flat water in front of them. With easy skill the fisherman steered the boat through the passage and into safety on the far side.

"Gosh," said Tom. "That was clever."

"Been doing it since I was a lad. We'll turn west here and drop me pots further along the reef. I'm trying a new place. Those bastards back in the harbour think they know my marks, but I'll trick them this time. We'll pick up the other pots on the way back."

He continued running the boat along the edge of the reef for what seemed to the boys a very long time. They had almost had enough of this adventure. The breeze was stiffening briskly when the fisherman called out at last.

"Now, when I say 'Let her go', you drop the anchor."

Tom stood poised, the anchor held ready and, as the man cut the engine and shouted, he flung the anchor overboard with a great splash.

"You didn't have to bath us all."

He threw over one pot, they moved on and he threw the second, Tom being more sedate with the anchor the second time.

"We'll get the others now. They're a couple of miles back. Don't pull up the anchor till I've got the engine started — we're pretty near the reef here."

He tugged on the starter cord, but the engine was obstinate. After several attempts the old man began swearing. He adjusted the choke, tried different methods unsuccessfully and again swore.

"It's that bloody plug. I knew it was dicky. I'll have to take it out — pass me that tool box there."

He cleaned the plug and replaced it, muttering to himself all the time. The boys crouched quietly. He was not quite so nice now and they dared not say a word.

"The bloody thing'd better go now."

He pulled the cord again with no response. Gradually a kind of frenzy came upon him. He pulled and tugged over and over again, and still the engine would not start. He paused, fiddling with this and that, then heaved harder and faster. His breath was coming in wheezing gulps now and the veins stood out on his red and sweating forehead. He gave one last great haul: the engine fired briefly, stopping even as it did so, and the old man fell unconscious across Giles' knees.

At first Giles did not understand what had happened, but when he did he called urgently to Tom.

"Quick, help me, he's sick."

They tried to put him in a more comfortable position, but he was heavy and it was difficult in the cramped conditions of the boat. Tom dipped his handkerchief in the sea and wiped the man's face; his head lolled and a little dribble of froth ran from the side of his mouth.

"Whatever will we do?" The words came out as a wail. They were both very frightened and frightened to admit it.

"Nothing. We'll have to wait till somebody comes." Giles was being sensible.

They sat still for a short while, which seemed an eternity.

"How will anyone know?" asked Tom.

"Of course they will. Somebody'll know. Don't worry." Giles adopted a superior tone in order to reassure himself.

"Can't we row back?"

"We can't — we couldn't get through the reef."

They both knew this was true. They must stay where they were and hope that somehow they would be found.

"I'm cold," said Tom. Giles had put on his shirt long since, but now he took it off and handed it to his brother.

"Here, put that on." He knew he had to look after Tom.

"What about you?"

"I'm not cold," he replied, teeth chattering, partly with chill and partly with fear.

The sun was almost down to the horizon now, and soon there would not even be its last rays to warm them. The breeze dropped slightly with the sun. In the stern Giles found an old sack and,with a knife that was stuck in the gunwale, he cut a hole for his head and two for his arms, making a jerkin. That was better, though the coarse jute was uncomfortably rough on his skin.

"Come on — we'll do exercises with our arms."

That cheered them and they began to laugh and hit each other on the back, the boat lurching all over the sea. There was a sudden great jerk and they were moving.

"What happened?"

"Look," said Tom in a quiet pale voice. "We've lost the anchor. The rope's frayed through."

They were drifting.

"Quick, the oars. I'll row."

Giles knew what he had to do, and did not waste time. They had been brought up in boats from babyhood and he was a good rower. With speed he shoved the rowlocks into place. He knew he must keep parallel with the reef, never heading towards it, and though the boat was heavy for a boy of his age and awkward with the old man sprawled to one side, he was soon rowing strongly. Tom took a turn but tired quickly, so Giles carried on. He could still see the land clearly enough to steer in the half-light, but it was growing more difficult. His jerkin was chafing him cruelly and the skin under his arms was already almost raw. The lights on shore started to come on, but they confused him and sometimes he was sure he was going the wrong way.

It was very dark now and Tom whimpered.

"Don't cry," Giles said.

"I'm not crying," Tom said furiously rubbing his eyes.

"You have a go. It'll warm you up." But Tom could only turn the boat in circles, and Giles had to take the oars again.

He was aching so much now that he could not tell one part of himself from another, could not tell whether it was his arms or his back or his legs which ached. The old man moaned and flung his head about and they thought he was coming to, but he fell back into his coma again. Terrified that the tide would send them onto the reef, Giles somehow managed to keep rowing. When he was almost worn beyond his strength and losing all sense of direction, he noticed a faint glow over the land. It grew and brightened and up over the hills rose a full moon. With it some new power seemed to come to him. He could see now where he was going, and he managed to hold them on course. The old man groaned and muttered. Tom was dozing, making little sobbing noises under his breath, and Giles was overwhelmed with affection and pity for him. He must not give up. He had to get Tom back home, to Mum and Dad. The thought of home put a lump in his throat, but he swallowed it down. His willpower held and he rowed on, making little progress, but keeping the dinghy's head into wind.

His mother had struggled through the day. After she had showered, she felt a little better and remembered that it was her day to help with Meals on Wheels. She could not let her colleagues down, and she had to pass the day somehow. It was unfortunate that as she walked into the hall at headquarters, two women were standing there gossiping about a friend whose marriage had broken up.

"Hello, dear," they greeted her, and continued their conversation while she was forced to listen.

"Such a nice man, too. Of course it's always the children who suffer — if only they'd realise that. They say he's going to have them."

Something in her head seemed to explode; she had a physical sensation in her brain. She could feel it clearly and the shock waves spread through her body so that she flushed and sweated and trembled. She knew without doubt that he would try to take the children away from her. Whatever he felt about children in general, he would consider himself diminished without his sons as part of his background. As he had told her, boys need their father. He would do his duty to the bitter end.

The two women turned to speak to her and she had difficulty in making herself utter words in reply. It was as though each muscle in her face must be instructed how to move and she stammered and repeated herself. They hardly seemed to notice her trouble; they were shorthanded that day and soon everyone was busy. Her head ached with her churning thoughts, but she forced herself to go on working; she would be no better off if she pleaded illness and left. Finally, her last job was done and she was free.

She liked to be home before the boys returned from school, and hurried over the shopping for the evening meal. She never let the boys arrive to an empty house. But they were late; they must have missed the first bus. Tom always did dawdle. She made a jam tart, their favourite, for dinner while she waited, and then noticed that it was long past the second bus time. What could have happened to them? She began to worry. Should she drive to the school and look for them?

Then her heart stood still. Surely he hadn't taken them already, not just like that, without a word or a sign. He couldn't do such a thing to her. She rang the school, but there was no one left in the grounds, the secretary told her. She rang his office. His secretary explained discreetly that he was not there, that he had left the office with a migraine. What should she do next? She paced up and down the house agitatedly for a while, then telephoned her mother-in-law. The boys might be there. She and her mother-in-law were on good terms, though the older woman secretly thought no one quite good enough for her only son. They were not close enough, however, for the younger woman to confide in her, so she asked about her health.

"My cold's a lot better today, thank you, dear. How kind of you to ring. How are the boys? It was the swimming sports this afternoon, wasn't it?"

She finished the conversation somehow. What a bad mother she was becoming; she had quite forgotten the sports. Perhaps the children were still at the pool. She got out the car and went to look for them, but the place was deserted and the gates locked. She searched up and down every street along which they might have walked and found no sign of them. Back at home she tried to think of any other possibility. She rang the dentist's surgery to see if the boys had had to return for treatment after school, but their teeth had been as perfect as usual.

He must have picked them up from school; there was no other explanation. All the talk of a migraine was a poor disguise.

The light was nearly gone. She sat in an armchair for a long time, staring at nothing but listening to sounds, as though she was expecting the boys to arrive home as usual, noisy and untidy.

At last she forced herself to eat some sort of meal and drank some wine which, in her nervous state, made her head swim. She flung herself across her bed, too giddy to stand up. Tears caught at her and, lying there, she wept, choking, sobbing, desperate. Unaware of what she did she fell into a deep sleep. Her last waking thought was to wonder where he had taken the children.

On his boat her husband was tidying away a few oddments, about to pour himself a drink. He was still trying to make up his mind what to do next. He had even tried ringing his wife. He needed to make contact with her. When she did not answer he was relieved, because he had not known what he was going to say. If she had hung up on him, everything would have been much worse.

He hardly noticed the sound of a powerful boat pulling alongside.

"Hoy there, anyone aboard?" came a shout.

Hurrying on deck he saw that the voice came from his old friend, the Fisheries Inspector who, after telling his offsider to take charge of the boat, came aboard.

"Have you got your boys with you?"

"Of course not. They're at home."

"Are you sure?"

"Why?"

"I don't want to worry you, but I think they're down here somewhere. Hey, Ted, throw over that bag, would you?"

A satchel flew through the air. The Inspector caught it deftly and pulled up the flap.

Tom's name and address were written there in uneven script, the address ending in The Universe.

"Where did you get that?"

"Someone found the bags and some clothes on the beach and gave them to me. Just let me tell you the whole story. There's an old boy who goes out after crays — he went off this afternoon, and told his wife he'd be back early. There's a family wedding or something he wouldn't have missed. When he was two hours late his wife rang me and I went down to the jetty. Two or three chaps saw him go off and they said he had two boys on board. Fair-haired lads about ten, they said. Then someone found all these things under a rock and showed me. It sounds like your boys."

The man was bewildered as much as alarmed. What was his wife doing, bringing the children all the way down here? Was she trying to hide them from him?

"What do we do now?" he asked.

"I know where the old chap sets his pots, and there's just time, if we're quick, to get through the reef in daylight. If we find them, we can come in further up the coast. Have you got enough fuel to bring your boat? We'll have a wider coverage between us."

"I've got plenty."

Only just beginning to grasp the fact that his sons might be in danger, he followed the big launch. He knew about the break in the reef, and needed all his concentration to navigate it. The light was failing fast now and the search began in earnest. In the old man's usual fishing spot they found two buoys which marked the pots in the sea below, but there was no sign of his boat.

Now at last the man knew that there was real trouble. The Inspector brought his boat within hailing distance and they co-ordinated their plans quickly, taking into consideration the wind and the tide. Both boats had searchlights and the men swept up and down the reef in an agreed pattern, gradually moving their field further west.

If at one time the man had thought that the children were more his wife's concern than his own, now he knew this not to be so. The longer the search went on, the more his deepest feelings were engaged. He must find them, they could not be lost now, just when he had discovered how much they meant to him. They were a part of himself he had denied for too long.

The launch pulled towards him.

"Do you want to keep going?" his friend shouted. "How's your fuel holding?"

"Keep going, keep going. I'm right. I've got some hours yet."

"It's a long haul back round the far end of the reef. We've got to allow enough for that."

"We can't stop yet."

He was desperately determined that they must find them soon, and convinced himself that they must be just beyond the reach of his searchlight. There were false alarms and findings. They came upon some floorboards, but these were from a much larger boat than the fisherman's dinghy. An old coconut bobbing in the water looked from the distance like the head of a drowned child, and he was choked with relief when they discovered what it really was.

So bright was the searchlight's beam and so intent was the father on peering into the darkness beyond the perimeter of its light that he did not notice the moon rising until it was fully in the sky and the water brilliantly lit. This changed everything; they could see into the distance now.

Again his friend hailed him.

"We can only risk another half-hour. We'll come back at dawn if they're not back in the harbour."

Knowing his friend was right, he nerved himself for extra

effort, tried to will the boys to be in the sea immediately ahead.

"I'm coming," he kept repeating. "I'm coming, hang on."

Giles rowed in a stupor. His arms moved, attached to the oars, but now the oars hardly skimmed the water. His head fell forward now and then, but he jerked it up. Tom was curled in a little bundle in the bows. He was not asleep, but wrapped in a daze of cold and misery. He had tried again to row but was not strong enough, though for a time he pushed while Giles pulled. But the old man's weight upset the trim of the boat, and it was easier if Tom balanced it somewhat. Tom knew quite clearly that they might never get home. The thought made him extraordinarily hungry and he felt sick for lack of food.

The moon was helping Giles, but he was so tired that the lights on the shore seemed to be jumping up and down. Then they started to swing backwards and forwards. If only they would stop. They were muddling him, and he couldn't quite remember now where the reef was. His irritation woke him up a little and he saw the lights more clearly, recognising them at last for what they were.

He yelled.

"They're boats, Tom, they're boats!"

They shouted and screamed, forgetting that they could not be heard above the noise of the engines.

"Pull off your shirt, Tom. Wave it."

Tom waved wildly. There was a strip of yellow waterproof material in the bottom of the boat, and Giles waved that too. The lights turned away and their weary arms fell to their sides. Giles, feeling the dinghy running before the wind, forced himself to pick up the oars again. The blisters on his hands hardly allowed him to close his fingers on the loom of the oar.

He longed for sleep and imagined himself fallen overboard and floating peacefully away in the sea. If the boats had missed them when they were so close, he could not hope that they would find them again.

His arms were part of the oars and he felt he was independent, detached from them, as they kept moving backwards and forwards.

By contrast with the searchlights the moon's rays were pale and they felt they were surrounded by utter darkness. Out of the blackness the lights swung back. The boats were making another run towards them. This time, despite the risk, Giles and Tom stood up to wave. One searchlight blinked at another, and the two boats bore down upon them.

Some hours later Giles and Tom were in bed in the room they had shared all their lives. Tom was already asleep, but Giles was sitting up, dreamily holding a bowl of chicken broth on his lap. It was funny; the dawn light was coming through the window. He must have been awake all night. He had never done that before. It had certainly been a day he would never forget, and it had ended as strangely as it had begun. He forced himself to stay awake to puzzle it out. No one seemed to be behaving normally. To his amazement nobody had been at all cross with them and, instead of the punishment he had expected to receive, everyone had praised him, patting his shoulder and making a fuss of him. Dad had even hugged and kissed them both.

There had been a crowd on the jetty and an ambulance waiting right by the steps. The ambulanceman had put some soothing cream on his blisters and bound up his hands, which stopped them hurting so much. The old man had been carried up the steps and strapped to a stretcher. Tom and Giles had always wanted to see inside an ambulance, and now they had a good chance to look at everything. But then suddenly the excitement had worn off and neither of them really cared at all about ambulances. Dad put Tom over his shoulder where his head hung and nodded up and down, and Giles started to walk the wrong way along the jetty, until the ambulance man caught him and said:

"Come on. I'll give you a lift to your Dad's car."

Giles was sore all over and, if he hadn't been a decade old, he might have cried.

Mum did cry when they came home. She bathed them and put them to bed and Giles could hear her talking softly to Dad in the next room. He didn't quite understand, but he knew that they were having a day off from school again tomorrow and Mum and Dad were staying home too. He fell sound asleep on the thought; the bowl fell out of his hands and the broth seeped into the bedclothes.

THE FEAR

The green sports car skidded on the loose gravel of the dirt road, headed towards a boulder jutting up from the verge on the other side of the road, missed it by the thickness of a butterfly's wing, bumped across the corrugations towards a cock-eyed white post on the opposite side, sprayed it with pebbles and slid on its way. The woman at the wheel corrected the skid automatically and brought the car under control, as she would have done a sailing boat struck by a sudden gust of wind. She knew the car's capabilities exactly and was angry with herself for lapsing into an inept piece of driving. Her heart was bursting in her chest with the shock of it.

She sometimes wondered whether such assaults on her body were shortening her life, or prolonging it by forcing a strange exercise upon her heart. She did not court fright as do some people who need to live with danger, but a quality of fearfulness was part of her nature, born into her as if she had been endowed with an extra sense. By necessity she had learned to live with this dimension of her character, but all kinds of trifling physical activities could cause her unreasonable fear. She remembered as a child the terror of being spreadeagled on a rock halfway up a hillside, unable to move in any direction while all the other children capered up the simple slope with no difficulty. Finally one of them had taken pity on her and, by coaxing and encouragement, freed her from her invisible chains.

She exorcised many of her anxieties by deliberately taking them on in battle. When a friend invited her to fly with him in his glider, she immediately accepted, though she dreaded the fear which she knew would strike her as soon as she climbed into the machine. It did, but at that same instant she passed beyond fear and was released by the joy of the flight.

It had not been her destiny to stay quietly at home, a peaceful housewife. With her husband she had travelled in many wild and out-of-the-way places and sometimes the fears attacked her on these journeys.

She rebuked herself for being over-dramatic. She must be tired after her day's shopping in the city, two hours' drive away. She was nearly home and, a few hundred metres on, turned through white-painted iron gates permanently open on a drive lined with lemon-scented gums and leading to the square stone house which she and her husband had designed in the early days of their marriage. It stood at the heart of the property, occupying a portion of the land which had belonged to her family for generations. She ran the place herself with the help of a stockily built workman who knew the land as well as she. Her husband was an agricultural adviser and worked in the nearest town, sixteen kilometres away. He was a solid man, almost rough looking, but his subtle hands and sensitive smile betrayed his deeper nature. A man of many interests, he was distinguished in his field, and governments of many countries called for his advice.

With relief she pulled up at the front door and went into the house, her arms laden with parcels. She dumped them on the kitchen table. She hated shopping, though it was supposed to be one of a woman's pleasures, and was always wrung out on her return from the tawdriness and facile salesmanship of the big shops. She always had the same need, after arriving home on one of these days, to go into every room of the house, to soak herself in its atmosphere. It assumed a life of its own while she was away; the light changed, invisible dust fell and the petals of the flowers in the vases moved their position. It grew away from her and she had to renew her dominion. Beautiful in her way, this was her own true place, the place where she was fulfilled and at ease, where she could allow herself to open out with no reservations and with no need of protection from an intrusive world. Here was no withdrawing within herself to avoid too intimate an approach from strangers, but an acceptance of everything that life brought her, all the richness pouring from her love of her family and the land. Here she could carry out the full variety of her pursuits, turning over in her mind every morning which one she must attend to that day, savouring the thoughts like treasures to be sorted. This was her fortress and she defended its privacy, having a great distaste for allowing anyone but her chosen friends within its bounds. She resisted the pollution of inviting someone to the house merely as a matter of form or for reasons of expediency. There must be a warmth between anyone within its walls, and within it there could be no fear.

Her children, grown-up now, had left home but returned frequently, and their bedrooms were still full of the strange mixture of treasures which they had accumulated through their lifetimes. The very scent of the children hung there; her daughter's room held a light fragrance, her son's something more exotic, harder to define.

She flung open windows, threw out a bunch of dead roses and gradually became mistress of her own house again. Returning to the kitchen she unpacked her parcels. There was always a small frisson of excitement over this; amongst the dull necessities there was always some treat, some little present for her husband, a new kind of cheese perhaps, a book he had mentioned. Today she unwrapped a glass figure of a cat, a tiny, charming thing which she had noticed by chance in a shop window. She and her husband frequently read aloud to each other; last night he had read her the story of Matthew Flinders' cat Trim, and this gift had seemed appropriate. Carrying it to their bedroom in order to wrap it attractively, she sat down for a while in her armchair set under the window and gazed out, half-seeing, at a red grevillea where two honeyeaters were having their last sip of nectar before nightfall. She began to long for her husband to return, to hear his voice calling through the house, to feel his presence filling the rooms. He must be on his way now, and her whole body yearned for him.

Gradually she became aware of a strange sound, a drumming. She could hardly place it; it was a regular beat that came from she scarcely knew where. Sitting still and puzzled, she slowly realised that it was the sound of her own blood pulsing in her ears. It made her uneasy; she felt as though she was eavesdropping on herself. She had never listened before to her own heart in such a way, but there was no quelling the hammering that came both from within her chest and, at the same time, from the atmosphere around her. She held her hands before her and then put them to her face, as though they would still the sound that was dividing her, shattering her wholeness. Standing up quickly she hurried from the room. She felt she must go about her normal affairs to rid herself of it.

Suddenly it was gone, not gradually as it had started, but in an instant and she was free from its thraldom. She could hardly believe that it had been so real and, leaning her cheek against the cold glass of the kitchen window, she took several long deep breaths, as though she had been starved of oxygen. Now everything was as usual, a pile of fresh vegetables, their colours clean and inviting, awaiting her on the table.

When her husband arrived she was cheerfully preparing a meal, weariness forgotten. He was delighted with her present for him, and she told him all her news. She usually made a point of seeing one or other of her friends when she was in town, so that the whole day was not entirely given to dreary pursuits, and she had snippets of gossip with which to entertain him. They laughed together all through dinner.

He was always a tender and compelling lover, and that night when they made love he was more passionate than ever. Afterwards they slept deeply in the peace of fulfilled love.

She woke in the morning before he did, which was unusual, for he had no tolerance for sleeping in. Luxuriating in a few extra moments in bed, she gazed at his head on the pillow, his black hair blurring before her sleepy eyes. His hair was so dark that someone had once asked her if he dyed it.

His rich thick hair set him aside from other men, and was his most striking physical attribute.

She had not thought to mention the strange sound to him the night before, and did not think of it now. Later, when he came to breakfast, she took pleasure in waiting on him more attentively than usual, brought his coffee to the table instead of allowing him to pour it beside the stove. They were well pleased with each other and parted happily for their day's work.

That afternoon she visited a new baby at the hospital, the tiny perfect daughter of a pretty girl whom she had first seen also as a tiny perfect baby, the new daughter of an old school friend, in the same hospital. She had picked with especial care a bunch of flowers from the garden, and wrapped in tissue paper a little smock she had sewn. There was so much to talk about that she was late coming back to the house. A thunderstorm was brewing; rolling black clouds were pouring across the sky, and she went into her son's room to make certain the window was shut.

As she paused to look at the lowering sky she again heard

the strange sound. Though it was the same drumming as before, this time it was louder, more resonant and did not seem to come from within herself at all. Yet still she could not tell whence it did come. There was nothing in the house which could produce so regular a sound and yet it surrounded her, filled the room, persistent and all pervading, as though the very walls of the house were the skin of a drum upon which a cruel hand was beating. Her own heart, her own house, seemed to be the source of her torment; she was betrayed by them. Terrified, she ran outside hoping to find there some remedy. Just then her husband drove up to the door and was startled to find her so distressed.

Holding her in his arms while she explained what had happened, he reassured her.

"*I* can't hear anything — it must have stopped now."

It was true; there was no sound except that of the evening birds settling. "It must have been a tractor going down the road," he said.

She tried to accept his explanation, but was still unsure. Nevertheless she again put the matter at the back of her mind. By morning she had recovered, and a busy day about the place took up all her attention. Nothing unusual happened that afternoon, Thursday. Her husband was always late for dinner on Thursdays. He played backgammon with a friend and usually returned slightly and amiably tipsy and amorous. She found him very attractive in this mood.

Tonight, as usual, he came through the door, calling, "Where's my girl?"

Swinging her round so that he clasped her to him from behind, he rubbed her nipples with the palm of his hand, a trick he had, and as she laughed at him, pleased, they almost fell into bed then and there. Foolishly, she thought later, they sat down to their meal, and afterwards he was too sleepy to think of love-making. She was wryly glad that she had a good book.

In the morning he left with a slight hangover, and suddenly she felt neglected and angry. Not usually bad-tempered, she sulked about the house, and when the workman came for instructions she was snappish and short. Ashamed, because she well knew that the backgammon game was her husband's only slight self-indulgence, she went to her piano, always a source of comfort and practised a Mozart sonata until her mood lifted a little. Soothed, she went into the garden to weed the rosebed.

It was the wrong time. The thunder which had been rumbling

around the hills for days had returned, and the clammy atmosphere pressed on her spirits like a stale dishcloth. She brooded as she pulled up red sorrel plants from the base of the rosebushes, easing the roots out of the earth where they had spread like knotted strings. The noise she had heard in her son's bedroom was not that of a tractor on the road. It was something else, something directly relating to herself. Just as the strange sound had crept upon her, she now felt fear seeping into her mind. It was not the stab of sudden fright which she knew so well, but something so insidious and disgusting that she felt herself coming out in a cold sweat, felt a nausea sweeping over her. She force herself to continue gardening and tried to drive away her fancies by turning her attention to problems on the property which had to be solved. But her mind was not her own, and she could not stop it hovering upon the unexplained menace.

Fetching some secateurs to pick a few roses for the house — for she must behave normally — she told herself that the threat of thunderstorms sometimes had an evil effect on people. But that had not happened to her before. She wished the lightning and rain would come and wash away whatever ailed her. And, just as she formed the thought, a wild storm of rain fell upon her. Lightning dashed upon the boulders of the hills, and rivulets and waterfalls began spouting almost as the rain touched the ground. Quickly gathering her fork and bucket, already soaked to the skin, she ran for shelter in the house. The wetting was not only a symbolic cleansing; she felt active and happy again. She had always loved thunderstorms and stood on the verandah to revel in the fireworks of lightning in the sky and the orchestral grandeur of the thunder and rain. Slowly they subsided and, shivering, she went to her room to put on dry clothes. As she did so she noticed that she had left the piano standing open and, by force of habit, moved to close the lid.

Then she heard the sound again. This time it was clearly coming from the piano; the strings were thrumming and vibrating of their own volition, replying to the voice of the storm. Unbelieving and not so much afraid now as fascinated, she crouched against a chair while she took in this extraordinary phenomenon. She had always known that the house had a life of its own.

With a last grand crash of the tympany the thunder ceased and rolled into the distance, and with its fading the piano also became silent. She dared not touch it but crept away to her room, cold and weak. Dropping her wet clothes on the floor, she crawled into bed, wrapped herself in the eiderdown and lay there staring at the ceiling.

Here her husband found her and, while trying to quiet her as she told the story, was half angry and impatient with her.

She could scarcely speak for hysterical sobs.

He was amazed that she took the matter so seriously. It was surely her imagination, and he rebuked her so that she began to rally in order to please him. Everything was suddenly so normal again that she began to doubt her own responses. Perhaps he was right; he must be, he was so sensible. No reasonable woman behaved in this fashion. She allowed herself to be comforted, though secretly she knew that the slow creeping fear was lurking somewhere, waiting to catch her again.

That night, as usual, he put a record on the gramophone but instead of his favourite chamber music he chose Mahler's 3rd Symphony, which exactly suited her mood. When it came to that part of the third movement which is so reminiscent of the Last Post, she was almost unbearably moved.

Privately her husband was much perturbed by her outburst and set himself to diverting her over the weekend. He took her to an antique shop which they had visited once before. Here they found a beautiful little Chippendale chair which exactly suited her desk, and they brought this treasure home. When it was put into place, it seemed that the house had only then been completed, so well did it suit the room. They were happy together over their prize. The house seemed to bloom.

Her daughter came to stay overnight, and the next day was spent cooking and sewing, companionably working together, talking hard all the while.

It was only when her daughter left to return to work, waving cheerfully, full of her own plans, that reaction set in and a great lethargy seized her; her hands felt too heavy to play even a few chords on the piano. She had always been happy in her own company, but now she craved someone else.

And then the noise was there again, faintly at first, then growing louder and louder, rhythmically thudding on her ear-drums. For a few seconds it receded and then returned to assault her, swelling, fading, and swelling again, the waves of sound pouring over her. The fear leapt upon her, filthy, soiling her even as the sound was polluting the air and the peace of the house. She knew that she must escape somewhere, anywhere, to leave behind the evil sound.

Running to the car, she jumped in, clumsy with the seatbelt in her haste. Inside the car the noise abated slighty, but it was still pressing in on her as she churned the self-starter with unnecessary violence and, throwing out gravel behind her tyres, drove away. At the gate she lost the sound and she turned north, away from the towns and hamlets, towards the flat mallee lands with the dry scrub and tufted trees she loved so much.

In the car the noise was gone and there was only the humming of the engine and the wind. Great stretches of flat, straight road opened before her, and she felt free and exultant. Here was the place to test herself and the car. Faster and faster she drove — 120, 140 kilometres per hour. The car answered every demand and was willing to give more — 160 km/h, 5000 revs. Scarcely time to glance at the instruments. She and the car and the road were united in speed. Easing her hands on the wheel she felt how well the car was holding the road; it needed only the lightest touch of correction, slowing as if by its own instinct for the occasional curves, accelerating out of corners. On and on she went, until the afternoon began to draw in and she knew she should return. But still she let the kilometre posts flash past her.

A farmer in an ancient Holden chugged along his rutted track to collect his mail. The old bus was pretty crook these days, no guts, coughed like a sick sheep. He stopped and picked up his newspaper and an advertisement for sheep dip. It was hard to turn the old girl round here; it was too narrow — he must chop that big bush down some time. Easier to turn on the road — there was never any traffic at this time of day, everyone home having tea. Without a look to left or right he lurched out onto the highway.

She saw him emerge from behind the bush a split second before she hit him. Even then she barely clipped his front mudguard. The sports car leapt into the air and tried to right itself, but the effort was too great and it rolled over and over, coming at last to rest on its wheels amongst the trees. The figure in the seat was motionless, slumped sideways.

The farmer stumbled forward to see the damage and, looking through the window, realised there was nothing to be done.

"Jesus, these cars are dangerous. They shouldn't let them on the road."

Climbing back into the old Holden, he drove home to get the missus to ring the police.

In the green car leaning against a tree a little flame flickered. Soon it became a roaring blaze and the two bodies, the body of the woman and the body of the car, were consumed in flames which reached to the top of the tree.

Not far from the square stone house a helicopter surveying for minerals banked beyond the hill and headed for its base, towing on a wire the box of machinery which collected its esoteric information. The helicopter had been patiently quartering the terrain for several days, the long sweeps of its search bringing it towards the house from time to time and then away out of earshot. Its work done, it disappeared now for good.

ONE SUMMER

The girl sat at the sewing machine, making herself a new summer dress. The rose-pink material moved easily under her fingers and the light in the machine shone on her face, heightening the colour of her cheeks, already flushed a deeper rose than the chambray she was stitching. From time to time a tear splashed down and made a dark mark on the material. She rubbed the back of her hand over her eyes and said fiercely:

"I will *not* cry over him."

She heard her mother approaching and bent her fair head over her work with even greater concentration.

"Clare, if you want to finish that dress in time to go out tonight, I'd better help you."

"No, thank you," Clare said stiffly. "I'm not going out tonight."

"But, darling —" Her mother stopped, puzzled. "Didn't you have lunch with Alexander today?"

"Yes, he took me to that new restaurant so that he could tell me that he wants to break off with me. He's got another girl."

"You mean — he said that to you — in a public place? And after so long —"

Clare was clinging to her self control with all the pride she possessed, but it was slipping away fast, and her mother tactfully left the room.

Clare dropped her sewing and went out into the darkening early summer garden. It was filled with the scent of lilies and the sound of crickets singing. A yellow rose caught the last rays of light and gave them out again like a lamp. She brushed the flower with her fingers and felt that stroking a rose petal was one of the most beautiful sensations in the world. Only better was the touch of skin on skin. She picked a daisy and began pulling off the petals.

"He loves me, he loves me not," she began automatically, and then, realising her foolishness, she felt her throat aching again with unshed tears of despair. The joyful summer she had planned stretched away before her, a dreary, empty vista.

She and Alexander had recently graduated as architects. He had been everything to her all through her university life and so, she thought, had she been to him until he had spoken so coldly and unkindly to her today. They had intended to carry out a project together this summer, before she joined a well-known firm of architects in the autumn. Alexander had not so far found permanent work; for an instant, a suspicion that he might be jealous of her hovered at the back of her mind, but she put it aside. She brushed her hair back from her face with one hand. She wore it cut short, like a little cap, and it curled softly round her face, but tonight it was almost unbearably hot on her forehead.

Her mother, preparing dinner, watched her anxiously from the kitchen window. Clare had always had a fragile quality about her, but now she looked particularly small and vulnerable and, standing there alone in the fading light was heartbreakingly beautiful. Yet she was resilient, as her mother well knew. During her childhood she had recovered from a long illness by sheer determination and effort of will. The illness had left her looking deceptively delicate and with the huge eyes which sometimes mark those who have known suffering. They were strange grey eyes, with deeper grey flecks in the iris, an inheritance from some unknown ancestor from whom she also inherited her strength. It was the strength of a wildflower, her mother thought; seemingly frail but able to live through storm and flood, raging heat and drought, to flower again.

Her mother longed with all her heart to be able to help her. The demands of children were so complex. Even when they were babies their needs were never wholly physical and, as they grew older, it became more difficult, not less, to fulfil their needs.

"As for Alexander —", Clare's mother thought fiercely, "coward!"

Viciously she slapped the meat on the slab in front of her with the flat of the cleaver.

A week passed. In order to pass the time somehow, Clare

redecorated her bedroom. Her two elder brothers were, mercifully, sympathetic and tried as best they could to rally her. Her father said little, but brought her the newest books from the library. Her mother cooked her favourite dishes. The whole household turned about her and she began to feel stifled by kindness.

One afternoon the doorbell rang and there stood her friend Mary. Mary, dark-eyed and lively, sparkling with energy and forever good-natured, had an intuitive compassion which responded at once to the misfortunes of others.

After praising the new colour scheme in the bedroom, she turned to Clare.

"I've come to ask you to stay with us in the mountains for a few weeks. That boy Bill I was telling you about is coming — Mum said I could ask him and he said he'd love to come; he's stayed in the area before and had a great time. And Carlo's coming too."

"Who's Carlo?"

"He's doing some extra degree and he's working with Dad. You'd like him." She paused, considering. "I thought you knew him. He's strange, somehow, different. He's exotic, like you," and she gave Clare a hug.

Clare felt a great lethargy. She had not the strength to be polite to strangers. All she wanted was to stay quietly at home.

"Can I think about it?" she asked doubtfully.

"No, you can't. We're leaving in two days. Say yes now, and *come*."

So she said, "Yes."

Her mother was delighted that she was to have a change of scene.

"How very kind of her parents to ask you! Usually they don't invite anyone to stay in the summer. Petrea's a wonderful woman — she has so many talents. She was such a quiet girl at school — no one suspected there was so much to her. Anyway, you've always got on well — I'm sure you'll have lots of good talks. I don't know Mary's friend Bill, but I remember his mother well. She was very sweet — they were country people."

"It'll be strange to be in the mountains in summer, instead of at the beach."

"Well, Hugo can't stand the sea and he generally gets his own way. That's why they built that house. I've known him so long, but I keep forgetting how distinguished he is these days."

"I find him rather alarming."

"I suppose he could seem that way. And who is Carlo? I don't think I've met him."

Clare explained.

Two days later the four of them left in Bill's car.

"Drive carefully," Clare's mother called after them.

A few days later Clare was walking down the main street of the little mountain town near which they were staying, reading a letter from her mother. It ended:

> *You have had a bad time and I hope this summer will help you. We were brought up to think that it was only possible to fall in love once in a lifetime. However, I am certain now this is not so, even if it has been true for Daddy and me. Perhaps we are unusually lucky, but one day there will be someone else for you, someone you can give your whole soul to. In the meantime, remember that we all love and support you and only wish we could help you in some way.*
>
> *It is getting late, and I must go to bed. Goodnight, my darling.*
>
> *All my love,*
> *Mother.*

It was part of the peaceful holiday routine to walk in to the town and collect the mail and the newspaper, and Clare enjoyed this. She already loved the little town with its road lined with poplars and its little old cottages left from the early days blinking their verandahs at the street.

Mary's parents had built a house on the steep hillside just beyond the town. Hugo was an attractive man, with a warmth and sense of fun which caught people on first meeting, but there was a suggestion in the line of his curving mouth of depths within him which he was only prepared to disclose to a few trusted people. He was a philosopher and, as an academic, had all the summer vacation, which he liked to spend in the mountains, for his own work. He was a vigorous and original thinker, whose books were read in Oxford and Harvard and whose theories were discussed in universities around the world. He was also an enthusiastic amateur botanist and would go for long walks in the afternoons, searching for new plants. These he would bring home to Petrea, who would photograph each one, then carefully press and annotate it. At the end of each summer they would take his finds to the Herbarium at the Botanic Gardens, and the two of them had now made a notable collection of Alpine plants. There was even one named after Hugo.

For Petrea this was her favourite time of year, a time of refreshment. She spent long hours on the balcony of their house, gazing across the valley with her embroidery or reading the classic novels which she loved and reread every summer; at present she was in the midst of *Vanity Fair* for the sixth time. She enjoyed them slowly, with a different sense of timing than that which prevailed in the city. In the city she was always busy. She felt obliged to keep up with the latest novels — this required fast reading or she would drop hopelessly behind. Here in the mountains everything was not only more leisurely but more contemplative. It was true, as Clare's mother had said, that she had many talents and photography was only one of these. Her advice was frequently sought by a variety of people, partly because she took a pragmatically broadminded view of the world, partly because her wicked sense of humour gave an unusual twist to any advice she offered. She was President of the University Wives Club and had often helped young and insecure wives.

She had been rather plain as a girl, her face too strong-boned for prettiness, and people had wondered what Hugo, was clearly going to be a success in life, had seen in her. But he had seen into her secret heart and had brought out the best in her, so that now she had the kind of beauty that comes to women who know they are loved. She enjoyed the company of men and they found her attractive. In town, circumstances forced the two of them to lead rather separate lives. They both had so many interests, though they were happiest in each other's company. In the mountains they were closer and each summer brought a renewal of their love. They did not usually have friends to stay with them, but this year they had been anxious that Mary should have company in case she was bored.

Clare was grateful to her mother for her sympathetic words but, though it had all happened such a short time ago, the affair with Alexander now seemed a closed chapter to her. Since being here, she had felt herself lifted into a new world. She had never been to the mountains before and had been immediately enthralled by the landscape. The majestic vastness of the views across the peaks excited and amazed her. The clear air tingled in her nostrils like scent, filling her with exhilaration, and she blossomed like a flower when the weeds are cleared away. Even the sounds and colours in the bush were different, the currawongs more musical and the parrots more brilliant than elsewhere. Everything that had gone before this time she now felt she had left behind, like a dress which has grown too small. She was translated into a new realm.

Mary preferring to lie in the sun and flirt with Bill, Clare walked alone today, but was glad to do so. She had always needed some time to herself. There was an elusive quality about her, recognised by her family and friends, and occasionally she simply withdrew from the bustle of everyday life. Here, when the friendly noises of the household became too much for her, she walked into the forest behind the house, disappearing as soon as she was amongst the trees as though she were one of them.

Suddenly there was a voice behind her, and Carlo caught her up.

"Fancy seeing you here," she said. "I thought you must have slept in when you weren't at breakfast."

"No, I got up before dawn and went into the forest to record the bird songs. I am a great birdwatcher." He showed her the tape recorder and the binoculars he was carrying. "I thought I might find you at the newsagent's, but I missed you."

He refrained from telling her about his conversation with the jolly, bouncing girl in the shop. He did not want to carry gossip.

The girl had said to him, "You got that chap Bill who was working up here last year staying out with you lot? He was working up here last summer. Give him a message, would you? Tell him Lorraine's engaged, and her boyfriend's captain of the footy club."

He had asked, "Are you Lorraine?"

"No, Lorraine's my girlfriend. If you'd just tell him that. He'll know."

Carlo kept this to himself, and said to Clare, "Would you like to come with me one morning and hear the birds?"

Her grey eyes lit up with self mockery. "Maybe. But I'm the laziest girl in town before breakfast. Later perhaps, I'd love to come."

"I think you'd enjoy it."

She was pleased to have been asked. There was something about Carlo that drew her towards him; a sympathy flowed between them. He had a dark quality to which she responded. Her fairness needed shadow to open out to the full.

They walked in silence for a while. Suddenly he spoke.

"You know, you're very beautiful."

She was not a child and neither was she averse to praise, but this was so unexpected that she was startled and her reply sounded sarcastic.

"Do you always say things like that to girls at this hour of the morning?"

He replied cheerfully, "Yes — it's my hot Latin temperament."

"Have you a Latin temperament?"

"My parents came from Spain, but I was born in Australia. They lived at the foot of the Pyrenees and they tell me I have the mountains in my blood. That's why I like it so much up here. This is a wonderful opportunity for me, you know."

He was very serious.

"Why is that?"

"My Ph.D. thesis — it's an analysis of some of Hugo's theories, and he asked me to come up here so that we could have some discussions about it. If it's good enough, I have a chance of a lectureship at the university. It's very important for me, because I will soon have to support my parents and it's the work I want to do. My parents are getting old."

She smiled at him. "I do hope you make it."

"Petrea and Hugo are wonderful people — they've been marvellously kind to me. They're the ideal couple, don't you think?"

She had not thought of them like that. "Yes, I suppose so, though I've known them so long. I think I still see them as I did when I was a child. I used to be frightened of Hugo once. He can be very fierce, you know. I once hid in a cupboard for hours when I thought he was angry."

"I can imagine that. There are certain people he won't tolerate, but I'm sure he would have been fond of you."

They walked in silence again. Carlo was not her idea of a dashing Spaniard, despite his black eyes and Zapata moustache. He was a quiet, gentle person and she liked him more than any man she had met for a long time. In fact, the only person in the party whom she found she could not like was Bill. Everything about him exasperated her. It was not because he was always teasing her; two brothers had accustomed her to that. It was his arrogance, and his assumption that he knew her most vulnerable points, and could pierce them, after which she would be appeased by his charm, which aggravated her.

She wished he had heeded her mother's words about driving. The brio with which he had attacked the road winding up the mountainside had not been matched by his skill, and there had been moments when she had been really frightened. Yet there must be something good about him, if Mary liked him so much, and her liking was clearly growing warmer every day. Affectionate, susceptible Mary. She wanted to catch hold of life and give it a good shake, and she found masculine charm irresistible. Certainly Bill was unusually good looking.

"I never did like curly hair, though," thought Clare disagreeably.

Every one of his remarks seemed to Clare banal and childish. Now she put him out of her head. She would write to her mother as soon as she reached the house.

> *Darling Mum,*
> *Thank you for your letter. I am better already. Truly. This is the most wonderful place I have ever been in. It's like nowhere else in the world and I can't tell you how much I love it all. The house is beautiful, built of wood and something like a Swiss chalet, but only because that's practical. The high gabled roof lets the snow fall off in winter, and the balcony upstairs catches the afternoon sun. Mary and I have a room in the attic. I've never been upstairs to bed before and I love the feeling of leaving all your cares behind you when you go up. As you can imagine, we have long talks in bed. Mary is a good, true friend and she has helped me a lot. In the morning when I first wake up I love to lie in bed and watch the curtains — white with yellow rosebuds — blowing out into the sun. It's all so peaceful. . .*

The days gradually assumed a pattern. In the mornings Hugo worked in his study, and Carlo struggled over his thesis. The others entertained themselves in various ways. Often they sat on the grass in front of the house, reading and talking. Mary, dark and bubbling, loved to lie in the sun wearing a minute green bikini, but Clare preferred the shade. She wore a straw hat which sheltered her eyes. Sometimes her smooth lids looked so heavy that it seemed she could hardly lift them to meet another's gaze.

There were two daisy bushes by the front door, a white and a pink. One morning she threaded a band of flowers for her hat, and then made a necklace and coronet for Mary. Petrea, coming into the garden with a tray of iced lemon squash, caught her breath at the sight of the two laughing, flower-decorated girls.

In the afternoons when Hugo went walking, the rest of the party would sometimes go on an expedition. There was a lake a few miles away where Bill had friends who owned a new speed-boat. They went water-skiing together. All of them, except Bill, were novices and he had a fine time on the first day showing off his skills. After that he was not so lucky. With his tall figure and long legs he was not built as an athlete, whereas Carlo's trim compactness gave him an advantage; soon Carlo was making dashing arcs in the water, swooping backwards and forwards on one ski in a way that Bill would never achieve.

That afternoon Bill spoke pettishly to Mary. "Who's that wog that your father invited? I don't know what he sees in him."

Mary was ashamed and embarrassed; no one in her family ever spoke in that way. But she managed to make light of it and persuade herself that Bill was trying to make a joke which had come out all wrong.

Petrea and Hugo always played cribbage before dinner. There was great rivalry and raillery between them, and the rest of the household would watch the game with interest, keeping a careful tally of the scores. It was something they all looked forward to.

Sometimes in the evening it was cold enough for a fire. Clare would sit in a corner and watch the flames, dreaming with her downward look. The warmth flared her cheeks, as if she were blushing at her own thoughts. But her thoughts were only half formed, rushing through her head like clouds at sunset, blown into shapes and then blown away again by the unseen wind.

She liked to help Petrea in the late afternoons with the plant presses. The paper in which each plant was pressed had to be changed every day, and the presses readjusted and put in an airy place to dry. It was a monotonous job and Petrea was glad of her help.

Working together was a good time for talking and she was easy with Petrea and could say what came into her mind. One evening, when they had just spread their paper on the kitchen table, Hugo appeared at the window, calling triumphantly.

"Look what I've found!"

They hurried out to see. It was a small, mottled plant, of modest but interesting form.

"This is the one I've been looking for for years."

He was jubilant. Petrea was as excited as he was. He kissed her ear and pinched her on her bottom, neatly clad in moleskins.

"Sex fiend," she said mildly and smiled at him.

"What's for dinner?"

"Rotton old stew."

"In that case I'll make a pot of tea. I was thinking of opening a bottle of champagne."

"Well, then, it's boeuf stroganoff to you, and we'll have the champagne."

Clare sat next to Hugo at dinner.

"I'm so happy you found the plant you wanted," she said in her soft voice.

He looked up at her, surprised by this first truly personal remark she had ever made to him. She went on to discuss his various finds, amazing him with the amount of knowledge she had picked up from Petrea.

"Would you like to come with me tomorrow?" he asked her.

"I'd love to," she answered, rather to her own surprise, for she was not a keen walker.

"I'll treat you gently," he said.

As the days went by and she grew accustomed to the distances, it was she who outwalked him.

From then on, the mountains were her kingdom and Hugo her guide. He knew so much, not only about flowers, but about trees and rocks and birds. He could make her see amongst the leaves birds which she had not even suspected were there; he taught her to stand still and to watch. She was enchanted when she found late violets in sheltered corners, their arrow-shaped leaves so different from those she had seen on the city stalls. She had never had a head for heights, but now she loved to perch on a bastion of rock, her legs dangling over a precipice hundreds of metres above the valley. The distant air seemed hung with blue veils of light, each darker than the last, each denoting a further range of mountains, all impenetrably wooded.

Hugo knew no fear and he leapt about the edge of the abyss, trying to see if there was anything unusual growing just below the lip.

They returned from their walks every afternoon glowing with pleasure at all they had seen and done. Hugo was a born teacher and loved having an enthusiastic pupil. He would pat Clare on the shoulder and say to Petrea, "This girl's learning a lot. I'm very pleased with her."

Petrea was pleased also. She knew the story of Clare's unfortunate affair with Alexander and, distressed for her, had suggested to Mary that she should have Clare to stay for the summer. She had thought it might do Clare good and was glad that her plan was succeeding so well. It was a joy to see the girl in such animated spirits, and to observe her delight in the place. Mary made the best of the holiday and did not complain but, secretly, her mother knew, she would have liked to be with all her friends at the beach. It was a boon to have Bill with them; Mary was obviously enjoying his company.

The only times that Clare deserted Hugo was when she went birdwatching with Carlo. She had taken up his invitation and they would go off happily together with binoculars to a pool amongst the rocks about three kilometres away, where dozens of small birds came to drink. The tiniest were her favourites, dipping and sipping amongst the ferns at the edge of the water. Honeyeaters sometimes hung from the blossoms. Carlo had made a shelter with a few leafy boughs from a tree, so that he could watch unseen. Here they sat for hours at a time, talking in subdued voices. They discovered a great deal in common; she told him all about her early illness and he told her of his difficulties with migrant parents. They shared confidences as she had not done even with Alexander. She talked of the work she hoped to do.

"It's a good idea to have women architects to design houses," said Carlo.

"Oh, I don't want to build houses," Clare said. "People

who live in them can do that. I want to design magnificent great public buildings in the cities."

Between them they planned an elegant city square.

Hugo grumbled and muttered complaints that he was losing his offsider.

"Go on, you're jealous," Petrea laughed at him.

Clare had never seen snow, except on distant peaks during their walks, so Hugo promised to take her to the highest point, where snow was still lying. One day Petrea gave them a cut lunch and they took the car as far as they could. On foot they climbed up to the snowline. There was only a little snow left now, in sheltered hollows and under rocks, stained with dirt and crisp where it had begun to melt and then refrozen in the night, but Clare was satisfied.

"Real snow!" she exulted, making a snowball, as she had always longed to do, and throwing it at Hugo. He was touched by her pleasure and pelted her in return until they were both breathless and wet.

"Enough of this," he panted at last. "There's a hut down below where we can eat our lunch."

They followed a line of tall poles, driven into the ground to mark the way in winter for skiers on cross-country runs. The day, so fine when they had started out that morning, had clouded over, and the wind was cold as they made their way round the shoulder of the hill and across a patch of reedy swamp. Just as they reached a clump of snow gums, a mist descended as suddenly as if a wet rag had been dropped on them from above. Hugo could hardly see the girl behind him, and certainly not the marker in front. He waited till she caught up.

"Now stay very close to me. The hut's only a few hundred metres away."

Slowly and cautiously they made their way forward from one pole to the next in the damp grey light. Hugo was furious with himself. He had allowed himself to do what he had warned his visitors against over and over again. He had not kept an eye on the clouds which had fallen so suddenly upon them. At last they reached the solid little hut. Built as a memorial to a young man who had died on the mountains in a storm and intended to aid those who were in trouble, it comprised one simple square room with a fireplace at one end and benches round the walls on which sleeping bags could be placed. There were emergency rations on a shelf and a stack of chopped wood in one corner.

Inside it was chilly, but it was a shelter. Clare sank onto a bench and sat huddled with her arms about her and her usual downward gaze. She said nothing.

Hugo looked about and then, seeing her so small and still, spoke gently.

"Were you frightened?"

"No." It had not occurred to her to be frightened. She had never experienced physical danger and she trusted Hugo completely. Hugo knew this and it made him feel even more angry with himself at his irresponsibility.

"No," she said, "I'm just cold."

"Here, I'll warm you up."

He grabbed her in his arms, in his jolly way, and began rubbing her back and holding her close to his own warmth. She was the child he had always known.

Suddenly everything was different. As he held her he knew that she was a child no longer; she was a young woman now and had changed in his arms. For an instant he gripped her more tightly, the blood rising within him. She lifted her eyes slowly to his. Then he broke away abruptly.

"We had better eat our lunch," he said.

Something so unexpected was happening to him that he hardly knew how to deal with the situation, and practical reality was the only recourse. Clare sat back on the bench, as aware as he was that everything was different between them, but uncertain as to what this might mean.

Hugo always wore an old tan sailcloth jacket on the mountainside, with huge pockets which held all sorts of useful objects. To Clare it was more than a mere jacket; it was a symbol of all they had shared on their walks and she was much attached to it. Now he produced from its pockets their packets of sandwiches. They ate in silence. They had always chatted so readily, but now nothing seemed appropriate. Neither could think of a word to say. Even the sandwiches were hard to swallow. Before they had finished eating, a ray of sunlight struck through the mist.

"Come on," said Hugo impatiently, stuffing the remains of his lunch in his pocket. "We'd better go. We can eat later."

Outside the air was clearer already and they could see some metres in front of them. An hour later they reached the car without difficulty. They exchanged nothing but the most superficially polite remarks on the way home.

For the next few days Clare refused to go walking. She was too tired, she wanted to spend more time with Mary, she must write letters. She did not even give herself a reasoned explanation for this behaviour. She had not committed her thoughts to words and Hugo did not try to persuade her. He seemed to avoid her and, if he had to speak to her, he sounded angry. He spent longer than usual working in his study and, when he emerged, marched off across the hillside without saying a word to anyone.

Clare was fearful of him, as in her childhood, but now she wanted to be near him. She longed to please him, but deliberately ignored him. She was in such a turmoil of confusion that she almost went home, but could think of no suitable excuse for such an extraordinary action. She was filled with a kind of dread, but scorned herself for being a silly emotional girl. Her pride would not let her show Hugo that she had made so much of what was probably a passing moment for him. When she was almost desperate, Carlo came to her rescue. He suggested that he teach her Spanish with the help of a little book of folktales he had in his bag. She accepted his offer gratefully, and the discipline of learning a new language rested her mind while the liveliness of the tales diverted her. They sat for hours at the kitchen table, Carlo pointing out nuances of meaning and instructing her in the intricacies of verbs and tenses. She hardly saw Hugo at this time. Apart from the ache of having to sit next to him at dinner, she avoided him. She would not even allow herself to catch his eye.

At last it was Petrea who urged her out one afternoon. In the early morning Carlo had heard a lyrebird in a patch of scrub that Hugo knew well, and he told him all about it. Though Carlo had not seen the bird, he thought it might have a mound nearby. Hugo was going to search. Carlo went off by himself.

"Do go with Hugo," Petrea begged Clare. "You'd love to see a lyrebird."

This was true; Clare longed to see one — it would be the crowning joy of her mountain adventures. After all, there was no obvious reason for her not to go walking with Hugo. So they set off. It was very hot and, instead of her usual boots and jeans, she wore light sandals with a thin skirt. Hugo chided her for not dressing properly.

"You'll hurt your ankle in those flimsy sandals."

She laughed at him and, because it was hot, went ahead and stood under the trees like a shadow. Then they plunged into the thick scrub. It was wonderful to be in the cool. As they crossed a tiny creek she saw some brilliant blue flowers shining against deep green, rushy leaves.

"How beautiful," she exclaimed. "What are they?" She held a head in one hand without picking it.

"That's dianella — it likes this dark cool spot."

"What a lovely name."

A few yards further on she stopped, puzzled.

"Listen — I can hear someone hammering in tent pegs. I didn't know you could camp round here."

He smiled. "That's the lyrebird, playing his mimicking games."

She was all excitement. "Do you think we'll see him?" she whispered.

Just then a brown-grey bird, trailing behind it a long tail clutched tight like a closed fan, ran across the path in front of them.

"There he goes," said Hugo. "Let's see if we can follow him."

Silently they made their way through the trees in the direction the bird had taken, but it was difficult to see more than a few metres ahead and, though they searched about for ten minutes, they could not find the bower.

"We'll only frighten him. We'll give up today," said Hugo at last.

Clare sank quietly onto a fallen log, her gaze cast gently downwards as ever. Her skirt was the blue of the dianella, and the curve of her body melted into the curve of the gum tree. Hugo sat at her feet, pulled fretfully at a tuft of grass, and then looked up into her face. Their eyes met at last and held irresistibly. Then he put up his arm and their hands touched and he pulled her down towards him.

"My little one," he said as he kissed her over and over again.

Later they said little, as though words might pollute this wonderful thing that they held between them. They walked hand in hand up the path and separated as they came out into the late afternoon sun. Pausing, they turned to look at each other, and he kissed her softly on her hair as they set out for the house.

Close to the clearing where they had lain, Carlo eased his aching limbs, stiff and cramped from keeping still and silent for so long in the hide he had built himself a little distance from the lyrebird's mound, which he had been more successful in finding than had Hugo.

That night it seemed to the girl that the whole house was filled with happiness. Hugo was unusually attentive to Petrea, who responded with lively gaiety. Clare felt she must make an effort to be agreeable to Bill and did all she could to draw him out. They were both guests in the house, and it was her duty to be pleasant. Bill was flattered and performed at his best, telling amusing stories about the months last summer when he had worked on a property not far from the town. He made the party laugh so much that their sides ached and they begged him to tell one more story. He was one of those people who flourish on praise. If Carlo was unusually quiet, no one noticed his dark looks.

Before she went to bed, Clare stepped out into the moonlight and, standing under a dark tree, watched the scene before her, silver and brittle as spun glass. She listened to the soft night sounds. Far away two curlews gave their eerie call. A little breeze visited her caressingly and then retired. She would never forget this moment in all her life. Her tumultuous thoughts slowly calmed and she heard a step behind her. Fearing, yet hoping, that it was Hugo, she did not move and arms went round her, clasping her breasts and swinging her round. It was Bill, who kissed her full on the lips.

"Don't you dare," she spat at him and, pushing him away, fled inside, the night's glory ruined for her.

She hated that young man but, washing her face with cold water in order to cool her cheeks, her rage cooled also. A kiss in the garden was not a crime, but it was unfair to Mary.

Mary was already in bed.

"I'm so glad that you and Bill got on well tonight," she bubbled at Clare. "He's asked me to go out with him this year. He's wonderful, isn't he — everyone thinks so."

Clare was half pleased and half worried. Till now she had known Bill only by reputation, which she now knew was justified. She had heard that he had caused a number of heartbreaks. She could not decide whether to say this to Mary or not. It would probably only annoy her and anyway, perhaps Bill had never been lucky enough to know someone as nice as Mary. Such friendships did sometimes improve a boy's nature. So she left it. Nevertheless, she thought his behaviour ungracious when he disappeared alone to the local pub towards the end of each afternoon, returning only just in time for dinner, generally slightly drunk. She was surprised that Mary tolerated his boorishness, but did not want to interfere and make trouble between them. He was sometimes aggressively rude, but even this Mary managed to excuse. Clare could only hope that, seeing him at his worst, Mary would realise that he was not the right man for her. Again she hoped that Bill might improve with Mary's sweetness.

As she was thinking all this, Bill was undressing in the room he shared with Carlo.

"That girl's a pain in the arse," he complained to Carlo. "She won't even give you one kiss. No harm in a kiss. I think she's frigid. She doesn't know what sex is."

"Who, Mary?" That was not Carlo's impression of Mary.

"No, of course not. Mary loves a bit of a grope."

Bill climbed into bed, feeling hard done by for the two minutes before he fell asleep.

Carlo lay on his back, sleepless for a long time, and gazed at the pattern on the ceiling.

Clair de lune.
Light of the moon,
Clare of the moon.

He repeated the words over and over again to himself.

From that day Hugo and Clare began their double life. They discussed the implications of what they were doing hardly at all for there seemed nothing to say. It was understood that Petrea must in no way be hurt. But how could something so perfect and inevitable hurt anybody?

Hugo showed Clare a hidden glade which he had found long ago and where he sometimes went to read. It was shaded by a shining white gum, the trunk as smooth as the skin of a woman's back. The grass beyond it was covered in mauve and white daisies. Here they would make love and afterwards she would lie naked on the grass, the sunlight dappling her pale belly, and he would read to her, taking a book from the big pocket in his jacket. Generally he read love poems, but one day he read her Andrew Marvell's *The Garden*.

"'Ensnared with flowers I fall on grass.' That's you."

"I'd better watch out — everyone will be wondering where I got my suntan," she laughed.

She insisted that they return each day in time for her to help Petrea with the plants. If they brought back fewer specimens than usual, no one was surprised. The season was drawing on and there were fewer plants in flower to be found.

There was never a hint of anything unseemly between the two in the house, no significant glances or light touches which might be observed. Clare could feel his presence in a room without even seeing him and chose to sit in the farthest corner so that she could occasionally look towards him over her book. Her very breasts ached for love of him, and it seemed to her that the air around him was lighter than anywhere else.

The days continued like this, a haze of bright summer glowing round them all, each day more glorious than the last. But as time went by Hugo had one wish which she would not grant him, however much he pleaded. He wanted to take her to the nearest big town, about an hour's drive away, to see the sights and have a meal together. She flatly refused.

"But why?" she asked. "It would be all wrong, and we have so much here. Why want something else?"

To her the idea struck a false note, and she was secretly superstitious that something might break the magic circle which encompassed them on the mountain. But he wanted to see her in a different setting, a new background to bring out fresh qualities in her and to enhance her beauty in a new way. Though she was generally amenable to his suggestions, in this matter she was adamant and would not be persuaded.

One morning while they were all sitting at breakfast, they noticed heavy clouds rolling across the sky. The air grew thick and stifling, as though the oxygen had been sucked away and there was not enough to breathe. When they tried to sit outside, thinking that it would be less oppressive than in the house, flies appeared from nowhere, crawling over their faces and into their eyes in irritating, disgusting masses. So they fled inside again. Over the mountains the dark clouds hung low and round, like plums hanging from a tree and about to fall.

"We may be nearer to Heaven up here," said Mary cheerfully, "but we're nearer those clouds too."

The weather made little difference to Mary's equable nature, but Petrea and Clare were both sensitive to its changes and fretted silently, wishing the rain would come and release the tension. It was so dark in the house that they turned on the lights and sat companionably round the kitchen table, but as the morning went by every occupation in turn seemed a dreary task, the muggy air was so enervating. Clare's magazine was dull, and she had no patience with the jigsaw puzzle that Mary and Bill were doing. Mary even snapped at Bill for putting pieces in the wrong place. Petrea was working at her embroidery, but the needle was always sticky and she kept running it through her hair to smooth it.

Clare picked up one of Hugo's books of botanical references. She was trying to teach herself some elementary botany for his sake.

Just then he came into the room.

"I can't work in this atmosphere," he said testily. "And it would be ridiculous to go out collecting this afternoon." He did not like his routine disturbed.

Clare pointed to a coloured illustration on the page in front of her.

"Is that a crinum?" she asked Hugo.

"Yes," he said and, leaning over her shoulder, said with an unusual emphasis, "It's sometimes called a Darling Lily. It would suit you."

Indeed, the white flower with its delicate pink tipped form, which yet had strength to withstand harsh conditions, was a most suitable flower for her, but she flushed at his tone. It was not like him to say anything so obvious. The storm was affecting them all.

Petrea looked across the table and folded her sewing neatly, smoothing the folds precisely as she did so. Carefully she collected the threads and put everything away in a tapestry bag.

"I think perhaps we should have a drink," she said. "Hugo, would you mix us some white wine and soda, please?"

It was a command and not a request.

By late afternoon the rain had still not fallen, and everyone was waiting gloomily for the storm. Even the earth was still with suspense. Hugo spent the afternoon making small repairs to the house, cursing mislaid tools and leaving the tools he was using just where everyone would trip over them. Petrea typed up her notes about the plants, the noise of the typewriter infuriatingly obtrusive, as though she were deliberately jabbing at the keys to make them sound louder.

Clare, possessed with the need to be alone, slipped out the back door and away through the trees to the forest above the house. Here was a huge gum tree which she knew well. All the summer it had shed its bark in the heat, until now its bare trunk stood glimmering, clean and pale, in the greenish stormy light. There was a round notch at about shoulder height; perhaps many years ago a bough had fallen from the place. It might have been the navel of the tree and she placed her hand in it, leaning her head against the trunk. It was as if she were feeling the pulse of the world and she thought she felt stirring under her hand.

"How strange," she thought. "This tree will be alive long after I'm dead and it's already much older than I am."

Then the rain began to fall, huge slow drops at first, and then a deluge. The scent rose strongly from the newly wet earth and Clare, loving the fresh, clean feel of the rain, stood still, letting the water pour down on her until she was wet through and her hair hung in dripping wisps round her face.

When at last she returned to the house she was wildly exhilarated, and she was dismayed when Petrea was angry with her for getting soaked. It was unlike Petrea to worry about such trifles.

"Go straight up and have a hot bath," Petrea told her abruptly.

"Really, Mum, you sound as though Clare was a baby," protested Mary, but Petrea was not to be laughed out of her irritation, and Hugo's efforts to appease her were not successful.

Clare obeyed meekly, but for a moment she almost hated the older woman; she had betrayed her trust. Gradually she regained her usual calm, but there was no recapturing her earlier mood. She wished she could talk to Hugo about it. But that was not possible, and she sat down to read in a corner of the living room. As though he knew that she needed consolation, Carlo came and sat beside her and, under cover of the general conversation, she found herself telling him the whole tale. He understood immediately everything that she was saying, and she found herself liking him more and more. Hugo sat and glowered at the world from his armchair.

Next morning Clare slept late. It was dark and there were no magpies to stir her out. She lay puzzling at some unusual sound and realised sleepily that it was the rain still pouring steadily down. All day it continued with hardly a break. The hillsides spouted waterfalls and streams, and the three men went out with spades and shovels to clear a drain which had become blocked. They were glad of the occupation.

After a few hopeful gold gleams at sunset the rain returned and continued relentlessly on the second day. It was beginning to prey on all their nerves, and that morning Hugo and Clare quarrelled. The sky had lifted a little and they both stood under the shelter of the eaves, watching the bright drops from the roof splash onto the ground.

"This is unendurable," said Hugo in a low voice. "We must get away — why not visit the town? This is a perfect opportunity."

"Of course I can't, unless the others come too," she answered. "Whatever would they think?"

"I don't care what they think, and I don't want the others."

The need to keep their voices low charged the argument with more tension and they ended by quarrelling furiously. Appalled, she suddenly turned and left him, hurrying to her bedroom. There she lay on her bed with her eyes closed, longing to go to him, to hold out her arms, to be at one with him again. There was no opportunity. She heard the door open and, imagining that it was Mary, sat up with some excuse ready. But it was Hugo and they clung together desperately, murmuring endearments while he stroked her hair.

"You shouldn't be here. Someone will find us. Thank God you came, I couldn't have borne it if you hadn't, but do go away now and I'll think about it."

As it chanced an opportunity arose which made the outing so natural that she wondered why she had been so apprehensive.

In the late afternoon Petrea, who was one of those people who are seldom ill and never spend a day in bed, was smitten with a violent bilious attack. It was as though the tensions building up in the house were too much for her and she had something within herself which she must spew out. By dawn the rain had stopped and her illness abated, but she was so weak and tired that all she could do was lie on her bed and try to sleep. It was almost a kindness to leave her in peace in a quiet house.

"Clare and I'll go off for the day," said Hugo to Mary, who was staying to look after her mother. Bill had disappeared early to visit his friends on the lake. Carlo was working in his room. So they drove away.

It was a day set aside from all others. The weather was perfect now, the sun sparkling but not too hot, all the colours brighter after the rain, the leaves on the trees standing out with vivid clarity. Their quarrel and reconciliation seemed to have brought them closer together. They had discovered depths in each other which neither had suspected. Now they delighted in the luxury of being alone together after being cooped up in the house. They sang and recited verses of nonsense rhymes in chorus. The car soared down the mountains like a bird and every now and then Hugo leant over and kissed her.

"Don't do that," she cried in terror, lest he misjudge a corner.

"Why not? I'm living dangerously." But he was a good driver and knew his limitations.

He was tender and funny all at once and she kept him amused and laughing with tales of her friends, which he found endlessly entertaining. Everything they saw — two little children making mudpies by the road, a white horse galloping across a paddock out of sheer exuberance, its mane flying behind it like wind clouds — seemed to have a particular significance. The beauties of the day were laid out especially for them.

When they reached the town, they explored and enthusiastically admired some handsome new buildings. They discovered a fine new art gallery and a mutual taste in paintings. There was one picture that Hugo particularly liked; its subject looked like her, he said. It was a Pre-Raphaelite painting of a pale girl in a violet dress, standing at a window reading a letter, with a glimpse of a garden beyond the casement. Hugo was happy to find that he could buy a reproduction.

"I shall keep it in my desk always," he said.

There was a good restaurant in the town and they had an excellent lunch and a bottle of wine. The pretty waitress was benignly amiable and seemed determined to do everything she could to further their enjoyment. Clare took a pink rose from the vase on the table and tucked it behind her ear. It matched her dress exactly. He thought she looked almost agonizingly beautiful and, reaching out, put his hand over hers as it lay on the white tablecloth. A torrent of feeling ran between them, and she thought she had never loved him so much.

Afterwards they wandered into the street, light-headed from the wine and the excitement. They went into an antique shop and rummaged among the impossible treasures. In a corner of a glass case he found a tiny silver vase, beautifully worked in the Art Nouveau style, in the shape of a lily. He immediately and extravagantly bought it for her; the lily was truly her flower. As they left the shop he put the parcel in her hand.

"My first present to you," he said and kissed her cheek...

"Don't do that," she protested, genuinely shocked. "Someone might see."

"Who would see us here?" he mocked her lightly, and he put his arm round her shoulder while they strolled towards the car.

"You go ahead," he said suddenly. "I'll get Petrea a jar of boiled sweets. I know she likes them."

Clare wandered on, unwrapping her parcel to admire the vase again. She was so absorbed in her own thoughts that she did not notice, until she had almost reached the car, that Bill was leaning against the bonnet, his mouth twisted a little. She jumped, almost cried out when she saw him, and with difficulty forced herself to speak.

"Hullo, Bill. I didn't know you were coming to town."

"Ah, I don't expect you would have wanted to give me a lift anyway." His gaze ran over her slowly, lingering as though he were touching her.

"Having a lovely time?" he asked, a leer in his voice. "See you back at the house."

When Hugo returned Clare was white and shaking, fighting back tears.

"Darling, what is it?" He was all concern.

"It was Bill — he was spying on us. It was horrible."

"Bill? Don't worry about Bill — there's no reason why we shouldn't be here. It's no business of his where we are. It was just chance that he saw the car."

"I'm sure there was more to it than that." She was not comforted. "There's something so nasty about him."

"I agree with that, the bastard. I can't imagine what Mary sees in him. Look, forget it. We must go home now and we're not going to spoil our day."

"Nothing could spoil today. Ever."

The long vacation was ending, but Hugo and the girl deliberately ignored this and refused to think of conclusions. The weather was unpleasantly hot and a scratching wind tore at the scrub. There was uneasiness in the air, and everyone knew without saying that it was time for a change.

One afternoon Petrea was working alone on the pressed flowers. Hugo and Clare were unusually late and she was irritable and weary. She saw no reason why she should attend to the dull part of the work while everyone else was out enjoying themselves. The kitchen door banged and there was Bill, swaying drunkenly. Petrea had been growing more and more concerned about Bill and Mary as the summer had gone on, but she had disciplined herself to say nothing, feeling certain that Mary's natural good taste in people would prevail. It had been a disappointment to find that Bill was not the person whom she had originally liked.

Bill stepped across the room and, grabbing her arms pushed them behind her back so that he leant over her. His breath smelt of beer.

"Stop that, Bill. What are you doing?" She was not frightened, but he was hurting her and she could not understand what was happening. He pushed her towards the chaise longue, which stood in the corner.

"Come on," he said coarsely.

She wrenched her arm away and shoved him in the chest. In his condition it was enough to make him reel back.

"Get out of here."

"Why, don't you like it either?"

"I'm married to your host, do you realise?"

"Married. That's a good one. I can tell you something about my host..."

Carlo came into the room so quickly and quietly that he might almost have been just outside the door.

"Bill," he said firmly, "I have a message for you. I met a friend of yours called Lorraine today with her husband..."

"Shit," said Bill and he lurched out, slamming the door behind him.

"Petrea, can I help you?" Carlo said calmly.

She made a great effort to respond to his calm and said in a flat tone which gave the measure of her self control, "Thank you, I would like that."

His kindness flowed round her like a soothing air. The only sign that something unusual had happened was her shaking hands, which rustled the papers as she picked up each sheet.

Bill somehow made his way upstairs and fell asleep across

his bed, one shoe making a dusty mark on his white bedspread, the other dangling to the rug below. He did not appear at dinner and even Mary was displeased by his uncouth behaviour. About midnight he woke, needing the bathroom. He heard the noise of doors shutting and people saying goodnight, but could not distinguish clearly what was happening. Staggering into the corridor he saw Clare flitting like moonlight towards her room. She went to pass him but he thrust out his arm and caught her.

"This time you'll kiss me," he said, clutching her to him.

She slapped his face hard and broke away.

"You *mole*," he mouthed, the schoolboy obscenity disgusting on his lips.

The next day was the last but one before the holiday ended, and Hugo and Clare took their favourite walk. As usual he wore his tan coat and in one pocket he carried the volume of poetry he liked to read from. When they entered the glade, she thrust her hand into his pocket, like a child raiding the pocket of some tolerant elder, and drew out the book.

"I'm going to read today," she said with a new tone in her voice. She found a sonnet of Shakespeare.

"'Let me confess that we two must be twain,'" she began.

But when she came to "I may not evermore acknowledge thee,/Lest my bewailed guilt should do thee shame," she was forced to hand him the book.

"You see, I am going," she said.

"I have to see you again. When?"

"No." It was she who was strong. "This has been our summer. Nothing will touch it."

She was trying so hard to say what she must without crying that a muscle in her cheek kept twitching, and she hoped he would not see it.

"I'm catching a train tonight. I've told Mary and Petrea already."

As the train was about to pull away from the station, Carlo stepped into her carriage. It was empty, except for the two of them.

"I'm leaving too."

They sat down side by side as, imperceptibly, the train began to glide out of the station, so noiselessly that it seemed as if the landscape was moving instead of the railway carriage. They were the only fixed points in the centre of the world. With a pitiful gesture she stretched out her hand to him and then withdrew it, her head cast down as ever.

"Why?" she asked simply.

"Because, you see, I am a fellow sufferer. I love you too."

At that she gave way and cried as though her heart would never mend, with her head on his shoulder.

At the house Hugo came to Petrea and asked dully, "What can I do to help you pack up tomorrow?"

"Nothing," she said. "I don't think I'll leave yet."

"What do you mean?"

"Just that. Mary can look after you — she'd like to drive down with you tomorrow. She says she doesn't want to see Bill again." Petrea offered no explanation.

"But we've got the Vice Chancellor's Dinner next week. You know how he likes you to sit next to him. I can't go without you."

"I'm afraid you'll have to. I haven't really recovered from being sick. I shall stay here until I feel . . ." she paused and drew a breath, "stronger."

They had been lovers for too long for him not to recognise every inflexion of her voice. He understood what she was saying, even if the words were unspoken. He held out his arms towards her, but dropped them. How often he had held and comforted her, but now she stood stiff and straight, beyond his embrace. He strode out of the kitchen and away across the dark mountainside.

"I love you," she whispered, gripping her hands so tightly together that her nails were white. The sound of his footsteps disappeared into the distance.

THE BLACK STONE

It was a strange episode. She never talked about it to anyone.

The garden was very overgrown in that place. Separated from the mown lawns and flowerbeds by a row of slender gum trees, it gave on to a disused orchard whose ancient citrus trees occasionally produced fruit too bitter and shrivelled to be useful even for marmalade. There was no water to spare for their nourishment nowadays, since pasture improvements had changed the water patterns. The orchard adjoined a stubble paddock, where a mob of sheep was gleaning the last pickings parched by summer's heat.

She came down through the garden, seeking refreshment after a busy day in the house. Though this corner was wild and untidy, with an old rose, its canes unpruned, setting snares across the remains of the path, there was a feeling of peace about it. Perhaps, she fancied; someone had once been happy there and the spirit still remained among the gum trees, drawn out by the sun like the scent which emanated from their leaves. In spring white narcissi covered the ground and she would pick crisp, scented bunches for the house. She loved the garden, enjoying all the processes of planting and tending, the feel of the earth as she firmed it round the roots of a seedling. She seldom bothered to wear gloves and her hands were constantly rough and stained. Gloves were such clumsy things; unhampered by them, her fingertips could tell a wanted plant from weed at once, or break a cutting from a shrub and tuck it into the earth to develop its own life. There was always some young growth coming on though there had never been time to attend to this corner; perhaps she would manage it one day.

She sat down wearily on an old wooden seat, half-hidden under a crab-apple tree and softly warm to the touch, its timbers grey and scored by the weather as if by a cat's claws. Her troubles were heavy on her shoulders like a thick black cloak and, as she half shut her eyes to rest, her husband's image, as always, rose before her. He had always been the source of her strength, the person from whom she drew all her courage and her nourishment. She had only to see him across a room amongst a crowd of people to feel renewed and made whole. Though she might be talking happily to a group of friends, his presence would eventually pull her irresistibly towards him. He was a tall man, of unmistakable physical power, and she had always been proud of his youthful figure, his skin smooth and taut as a boy's. He had a command of life which ordered her world.

Now it was she who must find the strength to nurse him and to see him through his days. Not that he was a difficult or querulous patient; he could hardly be called a patient at all. His illness might not have been discovered for some time had it not been for a visit to the doctor over some minor matter, which had led to further investigation. Now there was a tiredness, where once he had never been tired, and an occasional weakness in his limbs, but that was all. These days he left more of the station work to Bob, the manager, than was once his wont.

None of these signs might have alarmed her in themselves, but there was something she had noticed before his illness was diagnosed. The light had gone out of him. If she glimpsed him in repose, his face was grey and craggy, where once it had bloomed with enthusiasm for every aspect of his world.

As she sat musing, the garden began to work its magic and her cares to lift a little. She might, after all, remake these beds one day. It would give her something to occupy her mind, that dreary tenement inhabited by foreboding. She began to consider what she might plant. Lilacs, of course, several of them, their purple and mauve pillows seductive enough for a courtesan. Opposite them, ceanothis, trusses of the softest blue in the world. Beside the path many-breasted grape hyacinths and, under the lilacs, Lords-and-Ladies, their phalluses protected by papery green sheaths.

She was half amused and half stirred by her erotic fancies.

"On the fence at the end I shall plant Old Man's Beard," she told herself, laughing.

Just then she heard a step coming towards her across the orchard and was puzzled and irritated. No one on the place used that track; this was a backwater in the life of the station. She imagined that the intruder must be a sightseer. There were some historic buildings on the place, and she and her husband were sometimes plagued with inquisitive visitors impertinently demanding to go wherever their curiosity led them.

As she rose, she saw a man stop at the rough sapling gate.

"I'm sorry," he said hesitantly. "I must have come the wrong way."

"This is private property, you know," she replied tartly. "Are you looking for somebody?"

"I'm an historian and I've been told there was an old stone tower near here where some early German settlers once lived. I wrote to the manager to ask if I might see it. I'm sorry — I must have mistaken the directions."

She was about to answer, "You certainly did," but the quality of the man stopped her.

He was brown haired, a good deal younger than herself, deeply sunburnt and with extraordinarily liquid dark eyes. In this awkward situation he had a simplicity and directness which betokened absolute sureness of himself, and there was a warmth about him which even now she could feel flowing towards her.

The muscles of her body relaxed and she spoke with her usual courtesy.

"Of course, I apologise — you took me by surprise. Let me take you to the place — it's not easy to find."

He seemed perturbed at wasting her time, at taking her away from her resting place on the seat. He could manage very well alone. His solicitude was more than mere good manners, she felt, and his gentleness was as soothing as a balm. She responded and became animated as they walked across the orchard.

The tower, hidden in a thicket of elm suckers, stood on the far side of the orchard, beside a half-empty dam. The heavy squared stones of its walls were covered with ivy. There was one little room at the bottom, earth floored, and another above it, once reached by a ladder. Half a dozen solid hand-hewn planks were all that were left of its floor, and the ladder had fallen in pieces to the ground. There was no door, but a curtain of ivy hung over the opening which had once been the entrance and the only source of light. The afternoon sun shone through the leaves as if through stained glass as they stepped inside and gazed around at this rough home, where once a woman had raised her children. Thoughts of all that had taken place here silenced them both, and they stood side by side for some moments without saying a word. Unspeaking, they went outside and sat down on a fallen log in the little glade screened by elm suckers.

He turned to her suddenly. "You were distressed when I first saw you. I'm sorry if I intruded upon you at the wrong moment."

His unexpected directness, combined with the formality of his speech, startled her and yet went straight to her heart in a way that some more familiar approach from a friend might not have done.

She began to stammer some answer when, to her utter astonishment, she broke down and wept as she had not done for years. The man put his arms around her and held her firmly and tenderly, and she could feel no resentment for this solace, only a great relief as he gently stroked her hair and her shoulder, soothing, soothing, stroking and stroking again. She hardly made an effort to stop her tears, but gave in to the moment and let them flow away. Gradually she became conscious of the extraordinary situation in which she found herself, straightened herself and pulled away from him a little. She could not find it in her to apologise. With this man it seemed unnecessary. She told him, quite easily now, the cause of her sadness.

"You will feel better now." It was not just an assurance, but a promise that all would be well. "May I come again tomorrow? I would like to make a sketch of this place."

Automatically she replied in the tone she customarily used with strangers, "Of course, you are most welcome."

He gave a deep rolling laugh and, after a moment, she laughed with him.

"I know — I've wasted your afternoon. Please do come tomorrow and I'll bring some afternoon tea to make up for it." So they parted.

That night she found she had an unexpected lightness when talking to her husband and was surprised at how easily she managed to bring him out of himself. She told him part of the story of her encounter, and it interested him.

"I remember now," he said. "Bob did mention the man to me. I forgot all about it."

He proposed a game of cards, which had been one of their

pleasures in earlier days, and they drank a whisky and laughed and chatted until it was time for bed. It was the most pleasant evening they had passed together since the onset of his illness.

Next afternoon it was very hot and she put on a blue skirt patterned in white daisies and, instead of her usual rough walking shoes, a pair of white sandals. She took a flat straw basket, brought home with some difficulty from a visit to Brittany many years before, and carried in it a flask of iced coffee, some freshly baked shortbread, cushions and a rug. She was half excited, half embarrassed by her preparations.

There was no sign of him as she approached the tower, and a pang of bitter disappointment flowed over her. She chided herself for such silliness. After all, he was only a passing visitor and probably had a great many commitments. Then suddenly she saw him, sitting not on a sketching stool but on the ground, almost invisible, as if he were part of the foliage growing out of the earth. He looked up and called to her without getting to his feet.

"I've almost finished. Put the things in the tower — it's cooler in there."

Having laid out her little meal, she came outside just as he got to his feet.

"Forgive me — I just had that shadow to put in."

They stood looking at each other across the small space of rough grass. She knew then exactly what would happen. Dropping his sketch block, he stepped towards her and took her in his arms. She held him as strongly as he held her. She felt the skin of his belly tighten against her own. His penis pressed hard and upright and she was aching to receive him, her nipples tingling as they touched his chest through her thin shirt.

"Come with me," he said simply and, taking her hand, drew her after him.

They made love on the rug in the tower, a tiny breeze touching their skin like a stroking hand.

Afterwards, he lay back on his side gazing at her. Glowing, fulfilled, she rolled lazily towards him and stroked his loins with a finger. His penis lay softly against his thigh.

"You have beautiful skin," she whispered.

"That's my Aboriginal blood."

Astonished, she looked straight up into his eyes and realised the truth of what he said.

"Now I understand," she said. "That explains so much — I felt you were of the land, part of the land."

"My great grandmother was Aboriginal — she came from the west. I go and see my relatives there from time to time."

She gathered his penis tenderly in one hand and held it until it stood again and they made love once more.

At last he stood up and looked at her pale beauty lying naked before him.

"We must go now. He will need you."

She pulled on her clothes voluptuously, each garment another caress.

"Will I see you again?" she asked.

"I will come this time next week. I will come to the garden where I first saw you."

That night she and her husband made love deeply and satisfyingly, and slept clasped in each other's arms in the fullness of love answered by love. In the morning she was amazed to see a little light flickering behind his eyes. She could hardly believe that she had somehow lit a lamp there again. All the week she went about light-heartedly. He was miraculously himself again, or so it seemed. She could hardly trust the change; she herself was transformed.

On the appointed day, feeling her heart pounding like surf on rocks, she went down to the garden. He was there, standing quietly and only half visible in the dark shade of the crab-apple. She paused, the width of the wooden bench between them. They did not touch each other; a shyness had come over her and she felt only a tender gratefulness for all he had done. As they stood there, gazing at each other, their thoughts poured back and forth between them, without words. So many things they said.

"I came to say goodbye. I go home tomorrow."

"Yes, it's time."

"I brought you something. Hold out your hand."

Like a child, she put her hand out, palm upwards, and he placed in it a small round stone, black as basalt, polished to a shine by endless rubbing between his fingers.

"I brought that home from my country. I want you to keep it."

"But I couldn't," she began, and then realised how unworthy was such a response.

"Thank you," she said, and he turned and walked away

across the orchard. She was alone, bereft and yet returned to herself. For a long time she stood motionless, the warm air and dry scents of the place flowing about her. Suddenly, she dropped the stone into her pocket and, as if drying her hands, rubbed her palms against the side of her skirt and walked quickly back to the house.

With autumn she started work on the new garden. Her husband came and sat on the bench where he could watch her and sometimes he helped with her tasks. They were companionable and easy together. She marvelled at how much better he was. She had never hoped for such a reprieve. As autumn turned to winter he seemed to gain strength from the rain, which came early and plentifully. He was usually a summer man, but now he craved the cold and walked outside in all weathers. There clearly must have been a cure. The lilacs were planted, and one even bravely put out a small tuft of pale mauve flowers to greet the spring. They gloried over it together.

Nature was kind. One deceptive spring morning he walked out, lightly clad, across his paddocks to look for the new growth of clover. A cold little wind struck under his ribs and knifed him in the back. Two days later he died, spared the lingering misery which he would have had to endure.

At the time of the funeral she had no feeling. She had been told that he had died, she had held him in her arms as he had done so, but she could not yet accept the fact. He must be on a journey. He would return to her.

At the graveside they lowered the coffin into the earth on webbing straps. They had done it so often before, the attendants; it was their business, and all was professional and orderly.

She stepped forward with a bunch of white narcissus and threw them onto the coffin. Then she quietly dropped a small black stone after them. It made a little resonance as it struck the wood, but she was the only one who understood the sound. She turned and walked away so that she could stand alone and begin to know her grief.

SUCH A NIGHT

Lightning split open the night sky, making even the city lights dull. Rain poured down and huge drops flattened themselves into silver coins on the windscreens of late cars struggling to reach the dark suburbs through the storm. The drops caught the garish colours of the traffic lights, standing like tawdry decorations on the street corners.

The two women were driving home from the theatre, talking about the play they had just seen. Headlights glaring, a bus rushed towards them and doused the car with a chute of water so that the driver was almost blinded. She swerved towards the kerb and nearly hit a man crossing the road, almost invisible in a black raincoat. Recovering, she turned into a side street. "I hate these nights, Mary — anything might happen," she said nervously.

"Well, you'll be home in a minute and Tom'll be waiting up for you," said Mary comfortingly.

They stopped in front of Mary's tiny house.

"I don't know how you can bear to be alone in the house at night. Don't you get frightened?"

"Of course not," said Mary decisively. She had been asked that question before.

"I'll see you to the front door, anyway."

"Nonsense, there's no need for both of us to get wet. Here's my key all ready."

Quickly Mary stepped out of the car and opened the high wooden gate which closed off the house from the street. The house did not belong to her. She had rented it for a few months while her husband was working overseas, so that she could be near her married daughter and grandchildren. Their own house in faraway Queensland had been lent to friends.

Shivering in the wet night, she slammed the gate behind her. Even on a sunny day the little strip of courtyard, barely wide enough to allow a step up to the front door, was dank and colourless.

As she went to unlock the front door, she found to her astonishment that it was open just a fraction. In the wet winter the wood swelled and the door sometimes jammed, but she was certain that she remembered slamming it hard behind her when she had left earlier in the evening. She had even pushed it with her fist to make certain that it was shut. Puzzled rather than nervous, she swung the door wide open while she tried to remember exactly what she had done. Still more mystified than anxious, she went inside and turned on all the lights to make sure there was no-one hiding in a corner. The house was so small, with only two little rooms and a kitchen, that it was possible to see almost every part of it immediately.

The place was quite empty and, shutting the front door with a shove, she heard the lock click. She noticed a strange smell, something rather sour which she could not account for. There was nothing else unusual about the house; everything was just as she had left it.

She poured herself a nightcap and it occurred to her that her daughter might have let herself in with her own key to collect a parcel she had left for her. But there was the parcel, still sitting on the kitchen table. There was no explanation for the door being ajar that she could think of.

She tried to ignore the mystery and sat down at the desk in her room to write to her husband, though she still sniffed the unfamiliar scent in the air.

Her letter writing was an evening ritual. Sometimes when she was late home, it amounted to only a few words, sometimes it became a long account of the day's activities. She knew what stories amused him — how much he was entertained by her accounts of the doings of their children and friends, and how certain people's pretentiousness and snobberies made him laugh. During the day she kept up in her head a running patter of conversation with him, and at night she set it down in her letters.

He was a geologist, working now in New Guinea. Often she went with him on his journeys, and she remembered well a camp they had once made by the sea. She had thought the natives rather alarming at first and found it hard to distinguish one from another, but as she had come to know them better, she recognised the village beauties, the clowns always joking, and the practical, serious members of the community. On the shelf over the fireplace at home in Queensland she had some smoothly rounded pebbles and some ancient, battered, white shells which she had brought back from that trip. On this latest expedition there would have been no possibility of her camping with her husband; it would have been nothing but long days alone in a motel, so she had decided to come south to her daughter.

She was tired tonight and finished her writing quickly. She could seldom bear to end a letter — there was always something more she wanted to say — but tonight she wrote only a few sentences and, adding some words of love, signed with his pet name for her, put the letter in an envelope and sealed it.

"No more news till my next," she said, half aloud.

She undressed and went quickly to bed, but found that she was no longer sleepy. She read for a while and then tried turning out the light — perhaps sleep would come in the dark. But she only grew more wakeful. The storm had abated and all she could hear now was the rhythm of a dripping gutter. Each time she almost sank into sleep she would be startled awake by the beat of the heavy drops on the tin downpipe.

"One two three, one two three." A long pause and the drumming repeated itself. She pulled the pillow closer into her shoulder and stretched her feet. She could hear a fumbling, a breathing sound somewhere — there must be a possum in the ceiling. Now she began to wish that she had posted her letter — not that it would make any difference to the hour that it was collected — but, having put it in the post-box, her messages of love would already be on their way. As she lay there, the idea became an obsession, until she began to think that she might even go and take the letter to the box which was close by, on the corner of the street.

This was ridiculous — people did not get out of bed in the middle of a wet night to do such things. Then she thought that anything would be better than lying there prickling with wakefulness.

Making a sudden decision, she turned on the light once more and, getting up quickly, pulled a jumper over her night-dress and put on her raincoat and her boots. Taking the letter and leaving the lights on, with the front door pulled to behind her, she set off down the street. This unconventional behaviour was exhilarating; she felt better at once and hardly noticed the cold. The rain had stopped, but an occasional huge water-drop from the trees overhanging the path hit cold on her scalp. She realised that she had not combed her hair — what a sight she must look. Pushing the letter through the slit in the box, she turned back and half skipped along the path in her pleasure at being out in the night. The streetlights turned her uncombed fair hair into a halo round her head. So, dancing along the pavement, she reached her own door again, opened it cheerfully and from where she stood glanced into the bedroom.

There was a man lying, apparently asleep, in her bed.

She gave a small scream, and her hand flew up to her mouth to stifle it. The figure in the bed did not move. Half fascinated, half terrified, she tiptoed forward, ready to flee into the street in an instant.

The man snored, his breath bubbling slightly. He was clearly drunk, and the dyspeptic smell of bilious whisky poured out of his mouth. That was the smell she had noticed earlier. Spasms of trembling seized her as she stood stock-still, her steps checked. Then she crept silently forward again.

She was shaking with cold now and gingerly she pulled her warm red woollen dressing-gown from the end of the bed. This provoked no movement from the sleeping man and, gathering confidence, she took off her chill raincoat and wrapped herself in the gown. The shudders of fear which had shaken her when she first saw him began to abate, and she stood gazing down at the stranger, the blood beginning to liven her veins and speed her shocked thoughts at last.

She must call the police at once, before he woke. Switching off the bedroom light, she tiptoed quickly to the telephone.

What was the number? She must be quick, dial before he stirred. But, shaking, she could make no sense of what she was reading in the telephone book. What was this manual of how to behave in extraordinary circumstances trying to tell her? She could see the words but not translate them into action.

Then she paused.

There was something about the man in the bed which asked for pity, something vulnerable in his complete surrender to the circumstances of his drunkenness. She began to see him as a person, not as a dangerous object. He was in her hands and whatever she did might affect the whole of his life.

There was another strange circumstance. Perhaps because he was lying in an accustomed place in the bed, perhaps because there was something about the shape of his head, he reminded her of her husband.

Instead of telephoning, she tiptoed into the kitchen and made a cup of tea. She sipped it slowly, glad of the heat streaming down inside her and completely uncertain now of what she was going to do. She felt overcome by exhaustion. How was she going to explain the situation to a policeman? You see, officer, I went for a walk in the rain in my nightdress and when I returned I found a strange man...

Suddenly she was disturbed by the sound of someone struggling to open the front door, and she leapt up from the chair, dragging her gown around her.

"Who is it, who is it?" she called, her voice shrill with alarm.

"It's me, it's Jack," came her husband's familiar comforting tones and, with that, the front door opened and he stepped into the hall.

"Did I frighten you? I'm sorry — I know it's late." Holding her in his arms and soothing her, as she clung to him, he reached out one hand and turned on the bedroom light.

Then he pushed her away so violently that she almost fell. His face was white, his eyes dark as he looked towards the figure in the bed.

A long time later they were still sitting in the kitchen, where she had made him a meal of toast and scrambled eggs. There had been a good deal of explaining.

"The firm needed some new equipment in a hurry, and flew me down so I could arrange it. I didn't have a chance to let you know I was coming."

It had not been so easy for her to account for her reactions to the still sleeping stranger. Her husband was irritated by her behaviour.

"Well, we can't call the police now," he pointed out. "Jealous husband returns. I'd look a perfect fool. I'm going to try and wake him."

It was no use. The stranger would have to stay where he was until the morning. Jack was doubly annoyed.

Suddenly they both began to giggle at the whole ridiculous

affair. There seemed nothing for it but to pull down the sofa-bed in the sitting room and get some rest. Happy and warm, they snuggled close together and fell asleep.

Very early the next morning the telephone at the head of the sofa rang loudly, tearing into their sleep.

"Hullo," Mary muttered sleepily.

There was a silence.

"Don?" The voice at the other end sounded puzzled, then steely.

"This is Diana." A pause. "You can tell Don, whoever you are, he needn't think he'll see me again."

Mary put down the receiver. The room grew clearer, but her confusion remained.

Jack was now sitting up beside her and she told him what the girl had said.

"I've had enough," he exclaimed and, pulling his coat round him, strode into the bedroom. He shook the stranger by the shoulder.

"Are you Don?"

With obvious difficulty the man in the bed lifted his head.

"Are you Don?"

"Yes. Yes, of course I'm Don."

"Well, it's time you were out of here."

Sitting up painfully, Don dangled his feet over the edge of the bed. There he slumped, holding his head in his hands. He was younger than Mary had supposed, which might have aroused further pity in her, but somehow annoyed her instead. He looked so very sordid and crumpled. Young people were intolerable at times.

Finally Don pulled himself together sufficiently to begin to tell his story.

"I was drunk," he said. This was so obvious that neither Jack nor Mary commented. They radiated a lack of sympathy for this unattractive intrusion on their lives.

"It was my bucks party and I got so full that I thought I'd better not go home. I used to live in this house till a little while ago, but I gave up the place when I was getting married. It belongs to a friend of mine and I thought he said it was empty — I've still got a key. I don't remember coming in, but I remember hearing somebody. It must have been you. I think I was lying on the floor behind that couch. I don't really remember."

Mary gave him a towel and left him to have a shower. Later, she gave him the telephone message, as briefly and politely as she could.

"Thank you for everything," he said very formally. "You have been extraordinarily kind." He was now looking neater and more in command of himself. It was possible to think of respecting him again.

He still had some of the exaggerated dignity of the drunk. "I won't forget it. I'm getting married on Saturday and I know Barbara would be grateful too."

Stiffly he walked out the gate and off down the street, clearly struggling to maintain an even gait.

Jack latched the gate and turned to Mary, puzzled.

"I thought you said *Diana* rang?"

GOING TO STAY

It was a long drive to the coast and quite dark before they were halfway there. The car tunnelled along the dirt road between trees growing so closely together that at every corner they seemed to bar its passage, springing aside at the last moment to let them pass.

The man and the woman in the car had been silent for many kilometres. At last she gave a long sigh and he touched her knee gently.

"Were you asleep?" he asked.

She replied with a similar gesture, softly stroking his bare leg.

"No, just thinking. You know how I hate staying in other people's houses."

It was true. Warm-hearted though she was, she had so great a need of privacy and times of silence that the simple demands of courtesy that arose during such a visit left her feeling inadequate, unable to respond with suitable friendliness. As well, she was uneasy about redefining another's room with her own possessions, so that, even in her allotted bedroom, she unpacked the minimum of necessities and felt that part of herself was still shut away in her suitcase. She was ashamed of these foibles, seeing them as a weakness, but in her friendships she could only make a total commitment, not merely touch the surface of an encounter and move on. Besides, she thought, laughing at herself, it was unsatisfactory to make love in someone's spare bed; it was like imposing too great an intimacy on strange sheets, a strange mattress.

She had often noticed with what ease some women assumed conviviality, like the slipping on of a well-cut coat. She admired the ability as she admired adroitness in all things, but found it impossible to don such a garment herself. Other women could touch lightly on gossip, remember old scandals with amusement, and easily discuss the merits of the latest books and films. Chorally conservative, they could advise on the peculiarities of a new climbing rose, concern themselves deeply with each other's children and the virtues of certain acceptable politicians. She, on the other hand, continually tripped over the names of authors, misplaced newspaper references and failed to admire admirable pictures. But she knew the quality of a rose without remembering its name and, while she might confuse volutes with murexes on the beach, she never mistook the nacreous beauty of a Venus ear or the strength of a helmet shell.

With men it was easier. A glance across a table was a shared privacy. A few sentences aside in a general conversation were an invitation to a further exchange, in which she was the one who would set the bounds. This she did with a certain light-hearted mockery.

These opposing qualities of aloofness and warmth informed her most remarkable attribute. This was her glowing, tawny beauty which gave light to all those around her, a beauty so magnificent that it could not be denied or resented by either men or women. She was autumn-coloured, with a figure as rich as a peach. Just as it is good to stand in an orchard beneath a tree whose leaves have turned red-gold after their summer green, so it was a delight simply to be in a room when she entered with her smoothly graceful carriage. Her beauty was dependent neither on mood nor time of day. It did not rely upon the light of animation nor the virtues of dress. Indeed she was capricious in her clothes, sometimes preferring dark elegance, sometimes a peasant blouse. But whatever she chose to wear, it seemed the only adornment suitable for her.

Women sometimes asked each other, "Do you know how old she is?" But none could tell and she kept her secret, not from vanity, but because she feared the gods might strike her if she revealed a matter so intimate.

Her husband treasured her beauty in his own way. If a stranger made some comment, which often happened, the quality of her beauty forcing such remarks from strangers, he merely replied, "Yes, it is a gift", as though she were blessed with some remarkable talent.

His own tall figure stood well beside hers, and the same

stranger might catch a glimpse of pure devotion, mixed with laughter, as he looked at her. There was a quality about her which called for laughter in the way that the charming ingenuousness of a child does. Yet there was nothing childish in her, only a simplicity, an innocent eagerness in the completeness of her responses.

Her husband was a scientist with a deep love for music and a particular knowledge of romantic composers. This was the reason for their visiting comparative strangers for a few days. Their host and hostess were music publishers whose lives were set within the esoteric bounds of the musical community. The two men were planning a scholarly book between them.

In the car she moved again beside him and, replying to her comment, he merely said, "I'm sure you'll manage. You always do."

They drove on into the mystery of a strange road by night. No moon illumined the spaces between the tree trunks; a wall of darkness shut the couple in. A runover, with strainer posts on either side roughly cut from the trunk of some big tree, showed that they were nearly at their destination. Soon they drove through a gate to a house whose one light burning over the door made the building and the surrounding garden seem enormous.

At the sound of the car drawing up, their host opened the front door and, as they stepped inside, the evening and the house settled to a more normal scale. Their hostess was attentively welcoming, happy to have them there and immediately leading them to a verandah which, to their surprise, was only about a hundred metres from the sea. The soft flop and sibilance of the waves on the quiet shore had not been audible from the other side of the house. Returning to the living room, the woman noticed that it was mercifully free of driftwood, fishermen's floats or other beach bric-a-brac; only a few shells were a tribute to the sea. All was arranged for comfort and quiet living. The only eccentricity was the number of books to be seen. The copious shelves being full, they were piled in castles and turrets on the floor in front of the bookshelves. She wondered whether it was possible ever to reach those in the farthest ramparts. In one corner stood a cluster of fishing rods and beside it a rack held various firearms — a ·22 rifle, a ·410 gun and others.

"You look well-armed," she teased her host.

"I shoot a rabbit for the pot occasionally and the ·410 is for snakes. They come round the house sometimes, so you must take care when you go out at night. You might not expect them then.''

She shuddered. She had a morbid horror of snakes, a fear which went beyond normal caution.

''I hope I don't see one,'' she managed lightly.

They soon went to bed and, in their bedroom, still feeling the mystery of the night arrival, she determined to wake at dawn to see her surroundings by daylight. With the first light she sat up in bed, amazed by the huge trees which hung over the water. In the part of the world where she came from, the sea was edged by low windswept scrub. This pearly blue inlet, stretching away to distant rocks, was to her more like a lake than the ocean.

She looked down at her husband, his iron-grey hair ruffled on the pillow, his eyelids resting so lightly upon his eyes that he seemed hardly asleep. As she lay back he stirred slightly and flung his arm around her, holding her breast, and she fell asleep again in the warmth of his protection.

At breakfast they met other members of the party — two small girls of twelve years old, one a grand-daughter of their hosts, the other her friend. Physically the girls were much alike, with heavy fair hair framing flawless faces, and slender bodies not quite ready for women's clothes. Having emerged from childhood but not quite entered upon the awkwardness of puberty, their minds still held some childish magic, while at the same time reaching out to grasp the actualities of life. They had christened each other Holly and Polly for the duration of the holiday. Quietly and politely they sat at the breakfast table, spreading toast with Vegemite, occasionally rolling their eyes at each other and bubbling with secret laughter for the sheer joy of holidays and the nearness of the sea.

''You may leave the table,'' said their hostess and silently they slid away, to run shouting and laughing to the beach.

''Holly, Polly, Polly, Holly,'' they chanted as they ran.

On the smooth clean sand of the morning beach they wrote messages to each other.

''I like you.''

''So do I.''

They set about making a castle of stones which gradually grew nearly as tall as themselves.

''This is the mansion of a star. He hides here from his

adoring fans, waiting for the return of his faithless girlfriend. Here is the paddock where her three ponies live. No one has ridden them since she disappeared. Here is the garage for her Cadillac convertible and her limousine. . ."

Every morning they added more rooms, and the ramifications of the story increased with those of the castle.

The days fell quickly into a routine. After breakfast the woman's husband and their host went on long walks through the scrub, discussing their work. The still heat amongst the trees was oppressive to her, so she did not join them. Their hostess liked to spend the morning in the kitchen. Cooking was one of her great pleasures and she enjoyed preparing elaborate dishes. A few friends from the little settlement nearby usually called in and sat at the kitchen table, talking and drinking coffee, while she worked. The woman, as ever, felt ill-at-ease in this company and made the little girls an excuse to take her rug and a book to the beach where she could keep an eye on them. They had taken to her immediately.

"She's nice. Isn't she pretty?"

"She's got a beautiful voice."

"She likes lizards, she said so."

"She hates snakes, she's frightened of them."

So they murmured while she lay indolently nearby, scarcely troubling to read, soaking up the sun, her skin, already apricot, impervious to sunburn.

On the first morning, after lying awhile thus, she sat up and stretched, warm enough now to go swimming.

A young man, stocky and broad-cheeked, approached from the path leading from the house. She had been warned of his arrival. He was an art student, a protégé of their host.

"He's a good boy, a bit rough at the edges. He paints quite well. He'd like to see your work. I think you'll find you have a lot in common."

She was well-known for her exotic paintings of brilliantly coloured flowers, like nothing ever seen in a garden, which resolved themselves into animals and birds and seemed to hold an untold story in their petals.

The young man stopped squarely before her.

"You must be the beautiful lady they told me to look for." The pleasant words came out churlishly.

Her smile rippled up at him. "Is that an insult or a compliment?"

"It's just a fact," he said flatly, giving away nothing.

"Ah, but what is fact?" she mocked him.

"You are a fact."

"Well, sit beside me and we will discuss the facts of life."

He looked indignant and embarrassed, but his attention was diverted by the appearance of a boy who seemed to materialise from the sea, so sudden and silent was his arrival.

"I am Jason," he announced quietly, "I have come to stay."

She caught her breath at the sight of him. He was almost a man, yet still a boy. In her mind she called him a stripling. If her beauty was mature his was the antithesis. Slender and black-haired, his blue eyes were electric sparks beneath arcing black eyebrows. Despite his youth those eyes seemed to take in everything about her, to understand all that she was not prepared to tell, and a tiny smile of knowledge seemed to flicker over his curving mouth.

She found herself suddenly throbbing with desire. Startled, she jumped to her feet; the sun had lain too long on her belly and called for admission. She ran down to the sea without another word to her companions. The young man looked offended, the boy amused.

"Perhaps she doesn't like us," he said.

That afternoon she took a length of kitchen paper and some paints for Holly and Polly. Between them they painted a brightly coloured dragon, whose eyes were flowers and whose scales turned into fish.

The artist sat under a tree, sketching a rock formation. From time to time the boy Jason materialised in his extraordinary way, glanced at their work with his eyes half shut and then disappeared, somewhat to the woman's relief. She found his presence disturbing in every way. He seemed to be probing beyond her usual barriers, despite his silent manner. There was a current in the air whenever he stood beside her.

The little girls were ecstatically happy.

"Look, look. Look what we've made."

They proudly carried the painting to show their hostess, still presiding in her kitchen.

"Pin it on the wall here," she said and so they did, admiring their handiwork inordinately.

"Did you show the dragon to Jason?" their hostess asked. "You mustn't leave him out of things. He's my godson, you know.'' But Jason was seldom present at the right moment to be included in what they were doing and he never stayed in one place for more than a brief time.

So the days went by. The woman and her husband had always enjoyed each other's company and shared their interests and a multitude of small confidences, but now she saw less of him than usual. At night, after his long daily walks in the strong sea air, he fell asleep too quickly to talk about the day's activities. She reflected that she need have had no worries about making love in other people's beds. He seemed to have gone on a private journey, and she felt a little hurt and lonely. She knew he disliked sunbathing but wished that they could spend more of the day together. They were both keen fishermen and, though her hours on the beach were pleasantly idle she began to long for more activity and look hopefully at the rods in the sitting room. But he seemed to have neither time nor thought for anything beside the new book and the new intimacy with his friend.

On the other hand, she had gently tamed the young artist. They began to take more and more pleasure in their time together, making a little world of their own. Understanding as she did much of what lay beneath his surly manner, his own need to protect his innermost self which yet he must expose in his drawings, she could help him to accept both sides of his nature. Under her influence he allowed himself to drop his rough manner, and even his sketches gained a new freedom. They spent many hours talking on the beach while Holly and Polly ran backwards and forwards, sometimes pouring out confidences about their life left behind at home, sometimes begging them to come and play, which they obligingly did.

The stone castle grew bigger every day. It was the centre of their lives on the beach, and the myths surrounding it grew with its walls. At night in bed the girls told each other stories about the inhabitants, seeing themselves as taking part in its grandeurs. By day they held receptions and tea-parties, and the artist and the woman joined in.

Jason would appear and stand near them, though he seldom took part in their make believe. He was too old and too young for such games; his scornful beauty was unmoved by these amusements. She resented his brief appearances, the knowledge in his look as he stared down at her with a kind of suppressed insolence — so much so that she almost longed to strike him. She felt he was probing her precious privacy. As a live electric wire will not release one who touches it, he might entrap her in the same way, yet she almost wanted to reach out and touch him, just to see what would happen.

The artist disliked him thoroughly and said so.

"The little bastard's always snooping around. He watches over my shoulder when I'm sketching and drives me mad. I heard him boasting to the girls the other day about what a good shot he is. I'll bet he's never fired a gun in his life. I think he's a potential delinquent."

Though she half agreed with him, she felt it her duty to defend the boy.

"Oh, rubbish. I do believe you're jealous! Anyway, what you say isn't true. He told me his father taught him to shoot, and he's very proud of it. It's the only time he's mentioned his parents — they're divorcing, and I think he's torn between them."

Nevertheless a suspicion began to form at the back of her mind that troubles came to disturb their tranquillity whenever Jason was near. Holly and Polly, normally cheerful, began to quarrel.

"It's *my* turn, *not* yours. Jason says it is. He's a big boy, he knows."

She heard him in the kitchen one afternoon saying solicitously to their hostess: "What a pity Holly and Polly didn't like your pudding last night. It was such a good pudding and they wasted it."

She saw their hostess looking disappointed. She had not known that her baba au rhum had been too rich for the little girls and had been secretly disposed of in the rubbish bin. However, she had clearly forgotten his remarks as she pressed a second slice of pecan tart on the girls that evening.

The household was run calmly and peacefully. It was a benign place in which to stay. Maliciousness was quickly lost in the depths of its orderly goodwill and Holly and Polly flowered in its atmosphere. They competed to perform useful tasks, to run errands for their hostess, and were always bringing her gifts from the beach or the scrub. She accepted these offerings with serious consideration and gratitude, never condescension, and found a place on the shelf where they were displayed.

It was unexpected and irritating in this equable setting when various small objects about the house began to go missing.

"Have you seen my sheath knife?" the woman's husband

asked. "I always take it when I go for a walk and I know I left it on that table."

Everyone denied knowledge of the knife, privately blaming the general holiday untidiness and casualness. Holly's new green pen, a Christmas present, was next. Then cutting-out scissors were not to be found in the usual drawer. Polly's favourite book disappeared from beside her bed. She had nearly finished the story and she was sure she had not taken it to the beach. Each occasion produced a flash of anger and frustration and led to puzzled and unrewarding searches.

Holly and Polly added another room to the castle, called it the Lost Property Office and invented a tale about books and pens chasing each other through the scrub until the books took refuge in the castle, besieged by the pens. They fell asleep giggling at their nonsense but half expected to find the missing articles by the castle next morning. There was nothing but the footprints of a wallaby along the seaweed left by the tide.

One afternoon the woman and the artist went sailing with friends. She and her husband owned a yacht of their own and spent many days sailing together. She loved the feel of the wind and the sea beneath her hand on the tiller. Returning to shore after a boisterous few hours, she was exhilarated and salt-caked as she ran along the beach, her nagging sense of neglect quite forgotten.

She had paused to wave as the boat put out to sea when, suddenly as always, Jason stood beside her at the sea's edge and began skipping stones, at which he excelled. Straightening himself quickly and throwing down the pebble he held in his hand, he looked directly into her eyes and spoke boldy.

"Doesn't your husband like to be with you? Why does he always go off somewhere else?"

Furious at his impertinence and at his ability to touch her in a vulnerable place, just at the very moment when she had been feeling so carefree, she had difficulty in controlling her voice.

"He came here to work, not for a holiday," she replied nonchalantly. But her cheeks burnt red and she went up to the house immediately.

Later, at dusk, she and her husband went swimming, and it eased her to have a little time alone with him. She told him something of her experiences with Jason but not of the latest encounter, fearing that he might interpret it as a reproach on her part. He treated the matter lightly.

"He seems pleasant enough — he's a good-looking lad, don't you think? I'm afraid you've been left by yourself a lot, I'm sorry, but I've nearly finished the work and then we'll have a day to enjoy ourselves before we go home. You've been very patient."

Having no children of their own, he was inclined to treat children as a separate phenomenon. Their only child had been stillborn and she had been unable to bear another, a tragedy which they preferred to forget. It was a part of her life which she had sealed away within herself, even from her husband, but her loss gave her a motherliness in dealing with children to which they responded at once. It was not that she liked all children. She was as discriminating about her friendships with them as she was about those with grown-ups. Her feelings for Jason surprised her by their strength, and by their contradictions of attraction and distrust. She found herself thinking about him when he was not there and when she was falling asleep at night.

They were talking in their bedroom before dinner one evening. Her husband kissed the back of her neck as she stood before her dressing table, brushing her long hair.

"You're more beautiful than ever since we've been here. I think perhaps a lazy life suits you after all. Something here has done you good."

She turned, glowing, and reached up to kiss him on the lips. Then she went back to her dressing. As she opened her drawer she saw that everything in it was jumbled in a way she would never have left it.

Outraged, she exclaimed, "Someone has been at my drawer. Have you been looking for something?"

"Of course not. No one would go to your drawer."

"Someone has. Look at the mess it's in."

Though he knew her ways so well, he was not familiar with the order in which she put her clothes away and would not believe that anything so unthinkable could have happened. Nevertheless she went to dinner upset and suspicious. Something of hers had been violated, but by whom? Later she doubted her own evidence and decided that she must have disturbed the drawer herself in some forgotten hurry earlier in the day.

After dinner they played a hilarious game of Consequences. The party had never been more light-hearted, laughing tremendously at every joke. She was openly and appealingly flirtatious and all the men responded, their hostess, too, willingly beguiled by her charms. Their host produced some excellent port which went several times round the table. At last, still laughing as they called goodnight to each other, they all went to bed. She stood alone awhile on the verandah, listening to the voices gradually subsiding, letting the night air cool her cheeks and her tumbling thoughts and watching the ruffled ribbon of moonlight on the water. When she entered her room, her husband was already half asleep, his book fallen onto his chest.

She went to the drawer for a clean nightdress. She loved the feeling of silk on her skin and, voluptuously, she always wore extravagant underwear. As she lifted the shell-pink nightdress from the drawer, she noticed something odd and, looking again, saw that her husband's sheath knife had been slipped in amongst the clothes at the bottom of the drawer.

Incredulous, she gave a sharp exclamation of dismay. It was quite impossible that the knife should have come there by accident. Alarmed, she turned to tell her husband what she had found, but he was already asleep and she had not the heart to wake him, though she longed to do so. She held the knife in her hands and stared at it, as if seeking some explanation from it. The sheath was in place, fixed as usual to a leather thong. She noticed how the leather at the tip was wearing through with age and salt water. She laid it carefully near her husband's brushes and climbed into bed beside him. He was already so deeply asleep that he did not move, but it was a long time before she managed to fall asleep.

In the morning she woke early and unrefreshed. Thinking to have a quick swim she stepped quietly out of bed. She saw their host at the end of the verandah but went alone on her way to the beach. She needed some time to herself and revelled in the fresh morning, the tree trunks lit with a rosy glow and here and there a brilliant drop of dew on a leaf, fracturing the light into a multitude of colours. Stepping down the path, the low sun struck her eyes as she bent beneath an overhanging branch, and she almost tripped on a tree root standing out from the sand. Then she saw that this was no root but an enormous black snake lying immobile across the path, its little black head hard on the gravel, its tongue flickering. The ridge on its back was unusually pronounced; scale was angled upon scale and there was hardly a coil in the sinuous body. Terrified, she jumped back just in time to avoid treading on it, her heart pounding, her body trembling. Watching the creature closely, she backed slowly away towards the house, step by careful step. Then she turned and ran as fast as she could.

"Snake, there's a snake," she called piercingly.

Their host came quickly at her cry and, racing into the house, he grabbed the ·410 from the rack and put his hand on the shelf for the cartridges. His expression changed to bewilderment.

"Where's the ammunition, who's taken the box? Where's it gone?" In his urgency he banged the wooden shelf angrily with his hand.

By this time the whole household had been disturbed; everyone was running to see what was happenig, their hostess restraining the little girls from going outside. Their host, unable to find the cartridges, seized instead the twisted wire kept for such an emergency. But when at last he hurried down the path to despatch the snake, it had disappeared.

Everyone turned to consoling the woman, to reviving her crumpled beauty, to calming her. Her husband held her tightly, trying to pass off the episode as a trifle, but knowing how deeply disturbed she was. At last they all trooped down to the sea to swim, encouraging her affectionately, praising her bravery, until she was forced to laugh at herself.

"You really can't call me brave. I've never felt more cowardly." To relieve her nervous energy and divert attention from herself, she picked up several large rocks and added them carefully to the castle walls. They were now as high as her chest and solidly built. Then she chased the girls into the water.

A little later, as they were walking along the water's edge, returning to the house for breakfast, Jason appeared in front of them. He held a long stick in one hand and from it dangled the body of the snake. With the gesture of a Greek god honouring a chosen mortal, he flung it down at her feet, still writhing.

"I killed it," he said and strode back to the house without another word.

Breakfast was not a noisy meal that morning. A restrained atmosphere prevailed. Privately their host was fuming over the loss of the ammunition.

"It must be that new woman you got to come in and clean," he fretted to his wife. "She's tidied it away somewhere. You must speak to her. It could be dangerous."

Clearly some diversion was called for, and most of the party decided to go rock fishing at a spot some kilometres down the coast.

"I'm no good at fishing, I'll stay," said their hostess. Her husband wanted to look for an osprey's nest he had noticed once before near the fishing place; he might perhaps fish as well.

The party separated to prepare for the expedition. In their bedroom, the woman gathered up old sweaters and sandshoes. Her husband suddenly exclaimed:

"My knife! I forgot to tell you — I found it here by my brushes this morning. Did you put it there?"

"Yes, I did — you were still asleep and then the snake put it out of my head. It's all very odd."

Just then their host peremptorily summoned them — it was important to catch the tide. Holly and Polly bundled into the back of the station wagon with the rods and baskets, and Jason huddled in a far corner holding a bucket of cockles for bait.

When they reached the spot, beneath a cliff down which they scrambled with some difficulty, the girls ran away to explore. Jason was preparing to join the fishing party when their host declared that it was too dangerous for him. The tide was not far enough out, the waves on the reef were too high. Jason must join him searching for the bird's nest.

The woman caught the boy's look of resentment, but did not think that it was her place to intervene. As well, she knew that should her host's observations prove to be true, she was not physically strong enough to help the boy if he found himself in trouble. Her husband, unaware of the moment at which childhood's restraints become insulting, did not think to speak. The artist was simply glad to be rid of the boy.

So, after sorting rods and all the necessary gear, they tramped through warm shallow water full of starfish to the distant rocks of the reef, amongst whose gulches and caverns swarmed shoals of sweep and zebra fish, rock cod and moonlighters. The waves were breaking around their knees, and it was all she could do to keep her balance. But this was the kind of fishing she loved more than any other — quickly baiting up, casting out, waiting for the tremor of a touch and a quick strike.

With an eye on the sea rolling towards them from beyond the reef, an eye on the rushing sea below, they linked arms in support of each other each time a really big wave came for them.

She laughed aloud at the pleasure of it. The excitement of daring the sea, of watching it run in with white paws to grab her, added to the excitement of catching fish and she was utterly happy.

She was a good fisherwoman and hooked a big sweep, as large as a dinner plate. It gave her a great fight as she pulled it up, trying to run underneath the shelf on which she stood to hide amongst the seaweed. At that moment she doubted whether she would be able to land it, but played it carefully. The tip of the rod bent in a great curve. Winding in the line as fast as the struggling fish allowed, in triumph she hauled up the arching creature, silver darkening to pewter. She was terrified that at the last moment it might break the line or drop off the hook. Reaching out, she grabbed it firmly by the gills, managed with difficulty to remove the hook and stowed it in her basket. It was the best fish of the morning. She shut the lid of the basket quickly and pulled the catch into place. The fish continued to jump about furiously, jerking the strap of her basket hard against her shoulder while she called joyfully across the water to her husband. He was immensely proud of her success and shouted his praise above the noise of the sea. Full of hope and trying for one even bigger, she cast out again.

Her success spurred on the two men and they hung over the water, fingers sensitive on the lines, ready at the slightest vibration to strike and reel in. The fish, though biting briskly, were hard to catch, and yells of frustration pursued the ones which escaped.

At last they each had a good basket full; the cockles were finished and their shoulders were aching. They returned to the beach, chattering together in the good fellowship of the shared experience and the peace and warmth of the calm water.

Their host met them, thoroughly pleased also. He had been watching the ospreys all morning through field-glasses.

"Jason went back to the car to read," he told them. "I told him to take the spare rods — you didn't seem to need them. I'll take the rods, you carry the fish."

Together they scaled the fish on a rock beside a limpid pool.

"This is like a warm bath after those icy waves," she said, shivering slightly now that the tension was over, the wind blowing cold on her wet clothes. They started up the awkward cliff path, difficult enough to negotiate on the way down, and now made more difficult by the weight of their baskets. They were almost at the top, the woman leading the way, when something caught her ankle. Thrown off balance, she fell heavily, barking her knees and hands, sliding perilously close to the edge of the path and almost losing her load. Shaken, she picked herself up as the men quickly came to her rescue. Her husband was furious, unnerved by the danger which had threatened her. She was trembling with the shock.

"I don't know what I tripped over."

"I do. It's this piece of fishing line across the path. That boy is dreadfully careless."

On the upper side of the path lay one of the fishing rods and from it extended the line, weighted by a sinker, across the path and into some bushes. It had made an invisible snare which had trapped her while she climbed. Her host was extremely distressed, full of threats and anxious apologies.

She reassured him. "Jason must have dropped it. I'm hardly hurt at all — please don't worry." But, scratched and bruised, it was hard to put a good face on the affair and to appease the three angry men.

Jason was sitting in the car with a book. Ordered to climb out of the car so that his host might berate him more thoroughly, he stood silently, as always.

"I'm sorry," he said finally, politely enough, when the man ceased his harangue. Just then the smallest sneaking doubt crept into her mind. She was sorry for him being thus publicly humiliated, but there was an expression on that perfect face, a curve in that sensuous young mouth, which she did not quite understand. He seemed to be looking not at his host directly but just over his shoulder, in order, perhaps, to catch her eye. It made her uneasy, and she almost wondered if he were signalling for help. Yet it was his own action which had placed her in danger. Still trembling slightly, unwilling to witness any more of the unpleasant incident, she turned away towards the sea. Her husband touched her arm and helped her into the car. His gentleness brought tears to the back of her eyes, and she tightly clasped his hand for a second.

The sunny morning gave way to a disagreeable afternoon. There was a light overcast of cloud over the sun; a hot gusty wind blew sand to sting bare legs and drove dirt under the doors of the house. She wandered about hardly knowing how to occupy herself, nor where to go. Her husband and their host, with charts and notebooks, had taken over the living room. Her hostess had gone with Polly and Holly to buy stores. But it felt stiff and unfriendly to sit reading at the kitchen table, and it was the wrong time of day to lie on her bed. She tried the verandah but there was no shelter from the wind there. She decided to go swimming and to find a quiet corner amongst the trees where she could read.

She called to the artist. "Do you want to come?"

"Yes, I'll be right with you." She started down the path by herself.

So it happened that it was she who first saw the devastation. She could hardly believe her eyes at the sight of such desecration. The stone castle, the centre of so much thought and activity, had been destroyed, the stones thrown and tumbled in every direction. All the small treasures which had made furnishings and tea-sets and kitchen utensils were trampled amongst the stones. She felt as though she herself had been shattered along with the rocky castle. It was sacrilegious; the ruin of a dream. She walked about incredulously, wondering for an impossible moment if she could rebuild the thing, picking up shards of glass, pieces of bark and torn flowers. She was not yet angry — anger had not had time to grow in her. She was merely heart-broken and kept repeating, "Poor Holly, poor Polly," shaking her head to clear away the tears which flooded her eyes. How could anyone have been so cruelly destructive?

Here the artist found her, half-sobbing and holding between her fingers a tiny chair carved out of a gumnut.

So horrified was he that he stood in silence for a time. The sight was too appalling for shouted abuse or the relief of easy swearing.

"It must have been that little bastard. He's the only other person who comes here."

"I suppose so," she said in a small voice, shaking her head again and again. "I don't understand. I just don't understand."

Utterly subdued they left the ugly sight behind them and went to swim. The sea was cooling and consoling. Despite their concern at what had happened they both felt their spirits lift as they dried themselves. For a while they wandered among the trees looking for a sheltered place to sit. In a small grove of honey-myrtle alive with orange butterflies, she sank with relief onto her towel. It was restful to be protected from the harassing wind.

"This is better. You must take care not to get too sunburnt."

The artist laughed. "Not me — besides, the sun's gone under."

"But these half-cloudy days are the most dangerous, you know that. Lie down and I'll rub some sunburn cream on your back for you."

Cupping her hand with cream she began to massage his shoulders and then down the channel of his back to the point where it disappeared in a crevice at the band of his briefs. Her long fingers were firm and sure on his warm brown skin.

A faint sound made them look up. The artist, sitting up as he did so, found himself staring down the levelled barrel of the ·410. Behind the gun the shadowy figure of Jason was almost invisible against the dark trees.

"You dirty things — I know what you're doing. I'm going to shoot him, he hates me! You like him more than me. I'm going to shoot him."

The last brief words gave the artist time enough, and swiftly he lunged at the boy's ankle. The gun exploded harmlessly in the air, and the boy crashed to the ground where the two struggled fiercely, Jason kicking, biting, clawing and screaming obscenities. Though the artist was bigger and tougher it took him some minutes to subdue the boy, until finally he held him, panting and choking, tears mixed with blood and sand pouring down his face. The man kicked the gun aside and turned the boy to face the woman who was pressed against a tree.

The two beautiful creatures faced each other, both knowing so much of the other and yet knowing nothing at all. Suddenly she bent gently forward and held out her arms.

"Come here," she said softly. He moved towards her and she held him to her, comforting him with soft sounds, stroking his head and shoulders, crooning to him. The man picked up the gun and left them alone in the grove.

Next morning, when the visitors had gone, the new woman who came to clean the house was slapping a duster around the house and grumbling about the books on the living room floor.

"You can't clean behind them properly — that's the

trouble. There, see what I mean — a box of bullets on the floor. Dangerous things — must have fallen down somehow.''

She replaced the half-empty box of cartridges on the shelf and carefully wiped the barrel of the gun lying in its place in the rack.

WHY DID THIS HAPPEN TO ME?

The big hospital was particularly noted for its successful treatment of heart disease. It was also famous for the beauty of its gardens, which had been endowed by a benefactor whose wife had spent many years in the Special Wing, the ward devoted to patients whose crippled minds or bodies needed constant attention. The gardens were intended as a solace for these patients but, as if the perfection of Nature was too great a contrast to their flawed state, few of the inmates were ever seen sitting on the lawns under the groves of flame trees or beside the lily pools. Visitors wandered in the flamboyant rose gardens or admired the diversity of the succulent beds before they ascended to the wards, but benches grouped sociably under elms and pepper trees were generally empty.

The woman parked her car under a jacaranda whose purple-blue flowers had fallen to the ground, making a pool of blossoms which reflected those of the tree above, vibrant against a blue sky. The bees were busy both with the flowers on the tree and those on the ground, and she was sorry for her crass intrusion into their domain on this bright summer morning. Gathering her customary paraphernalia for hospital visiting — her embroidery, a punnet of strawberries from her garden, a bunch of lilies and delphiniums she had picked at sunrise, and one or two parcels — she walked, with her usual sense of foreboding, up the familiar path lined with magenta and pink pelargoniums.

Just then a line of nurses, smartly dressed in blue check uniforms, each pushing a wheelchair containing an aged patient, swung round a corner and came towards her, as neatly synchronised and jaunty as the chorus of a musical. Because she was a familiar visitor and any diversion was welcome in the routine of the morning walk, the chattering nurses stopped and greeted her, placing the wheelchairs with their charges in a circle around her.

As she greeted them, she tried to avoid using the affectedly cheerful tone of voice that the hospital environment tended to induce. The awkwardness of her over-filled arms made her feel foolish.

The patients did not respond. As they approached death they had gradually shed various physical abilities. Their legs no longer supported them, their powers of speech had failed. Only their eyes blazed at her, paler than the jacaranda flowers, but shielding thoughts at which she could hardly guess. One old man made a slight gesture with his right hand, a salute of some kind.

"There, he's a dear old thing, aren't you, love," his snub-nosed little nurse said, dropping a kiss on his fluttering white hair. The fierceness of his eyes did not diminish.

"Come on then, *off* we go — not long now to din-dins."

The woman stopped at a garden seat to rearrange her burdens. Her son was an inmate of the hospital. A grown man, he still had the appearance of a child and his achievements were those of a two year old. One of her parcels contained a small railway engine which would give him much more pleasure than her presence. He no longer recognised her and was more attached to the attendants who cared for him than to anyone else. She and her husband took it in turns to visit him once a month, as a duty rather than an act of love. Their own feelings had been harrowed out of existence long since.

She could remember him as a tiny boy, beautiful as an angel, with long fair curls which she could not bring herself to cut. He was their first child, and it was some time before the realisation that he was different from other children began to dawn. When the doctor confirmed their suspicions and urged them to place him in a suitable home, they were incredulous. The world had always seemed to them a hopeful place, where everything would come out right in the end. Because they were very much in love they were certain that they could overcome all obstacles and remedy every ill. Their principles forbade them at first to allow anyone but themselves to care for their child, but the doctor firmly overrode their doubts and persuaded them that this solution was best for the boy.

"But why?" they kept asking. "Why did this happen to us?" Bewildered, they felt guilty, as though they had committed a sin, yet they knew themselves innocent.

The doctor forbore to say that justice is a product of man's mind, not a fact of life, and that the concept of fairness and its rewards are generally limited to the boundaries of playing fields. Instead he advised them to have more children, which they did — a girl and two boys, all of them magnificently healthy and good-looking. They were never taken to visit their brother and only occasionally thought about him. Their parents saw no reason to force upon them a false concern for an unknown brother, and the retarded boy quickly forgot his early home and everything to do with it. He settled peacefully into his sheltered life.

Their daughter, now married herself, with two babies of her own, was a great source of comfort to her mother. Her commonsense helped her mother through the occasional difficult times which she still suffered over the boy, generally because she worried about her lack of affection for him. All her concern now went to her husband and to the other three children. For years she had recognised that her husband needed constant demonstrations of her affection to sustain him against the unreasonable feeling that somehow the boy's condition was his fault. The two had drawn always closer together and gradually her husband had recovered his self-esteem, as the other children grew and his pride in them increased. She was fully occupied with her family round, and happy to serve their needs.

She adjusted her offerings and, holding the flowers before her like a blue and white banner of freedom, took a long breath and climbed the slope to the big glass entrance doors which slid apart with a little clunk as she approached. Inside, the vistas of wide white corridors, floors glistening with polish, were broken up here and there with groups of blue armchairs. A few of the more articulate patients, who always grouped themselves in the large foyer to watch the flow of activity there, called to her as she passed. The stainless steel doors on the lifts gleamed a dull grey. Lights flashed and clicked and bells rang to indicate the arrival of the lifts.

In spite of the shining cleanliness, the atmosphere held the faintest scent of foulness, tempered with the smell of pine fragrance from an aerosol spray. It was air-conditioned stuffiness, a little too warm in winter, a little too cold in summer. Now she shivered in her light yellow dress. There was already a feeling of unreality — the artificially treated air and the bonhomie with which the staff treated the patients seemed only to make more menacing the hospital's mysteries.

An army of cleaners with electric polishing machines as solid and rounded as themselves moved constantly up and down the corridors, as though by sheer application they could remove the taint of illness. But they never quite succeeded, however hard they persevered.

When the lift came to take her to the tenth floor, she waited inside with patient habit, enduring the long pause before the doors closed. The pause was for the benefit of those on crutches or in wheelchairs, whose difficult passage across the threshold took so much longer than her own briskly unconsidered pace. In one corner a flock of dark-haired wardsmaids, plumply uniformed in pale pink, their hard-worked feet moulded by large comfortable shoes, trilled in Italian like starlings. One of their company leant against the wall of the lift, enjoying a voluminous cream bun.

Into the lift stepped a tall, attractive young woman, pushing an alert-looking baby boy in a stroller. The child turned his head from side to side, gazing with lively eyes at all the occupants, clearly expecting that they would admire him and possibly try to gain his favour with little blandishments and attentions. His mother, strongly boned and spare, a handsome blonde wearing elegantly tailored trousers and high-heeled sandals seemingly made of glass, was out of place in that setting. A tennis court would have been more appropriate, or a jet-boat tearing across the water with a crowd of fellows on board. Her clean good health and the buoyant spirits of the child were as cool as fresh linen in this place of sickness. Tossing back her hair, she glanced about with charming assurance and, possibly, with faint condescension. Her well-arranged life was not intended to encompass illness; that was something with which other people could be left to deal. She would bring up her boy with conscientious affection, the woman fancied, teaching him never to talk to strangers and always to eschew the eccentric.

As the lift moved, the woman's eyes were drawn to the wardsmaid who was biting luxuriously into a puff of cream and nibbling at the dough to lay open further snowy drifts. A red drop of raspberry jam clung to her lip and she licked it pleasurably with her round pink tongue. Icing sugar coated the tip of her nose. She looked merrily over the top of the bun, her black eyes enjoying all the world.

The young mother was clearly fascinated and she stared openly and obviously, as she had most certainly been taught as a child never to do. At last she could contain herself no longer.

"That looks nice!"

The wardsmaid licked one more creamy morsel and laughed happily.

"To an Italian, *all* food is nice," she replied and stowed the rest of the bun in her mouth.

The lift stopped at the seventh floor and the young mother, giving the woman with her flowers and the pink-clad wardsmaids a glance of farewell which dismissed them from her world forever, hastened on her way. She was followed slowly by another occupant of the lift — an ancient man, a mere pile of bones held together by a sack of tattooed skin. His disabilities were such that he could only propel his chair backwards, his head held at a right angle on his shoulder. The woman and the wardsmaids waited as he made his way out of the lift. The doors closed and they rose to their destination.

The Italian looked at the woman and, with a depth of sympathy which embraced the whole scene, said, "You can't help feeling sorry for them, can you?"

She understood well the good things of this world.

The woman smiled to herself. She would tell her husband the story of the cream bun that night. She was happy if the day provided her with such tales to amuse him. In turn, knowing her discretion, he related the office gossip, which always entertained her. She had several times been able to help one or other of his colleagues who was in difficulties, and was always pleased to be consulted for advice.

She did not imagine that she would see the young mother again, but she was wrong. Having visited her son and reassured herself that he was as happy as possible, she left him playing with his new engine, making loud train whistles as he ran it up and down a table. As she returned to her car, she was surprised to see the blonde woman tiptoeing with difficulty in her high heels amongst the brilliant pelargoniums, bending and poking here and there, clearly searching for something. The baby boy, unattended in his stroller on the path, was beginning to wail at such neglect.

The young woman looked up, her hair not quite as neat as it had been and with a few red petals clinging to it. On her face was an expression of mingled anger and dismay.

"It's my car keys. I've lost them. The baby was hungry so I came to fetch his bottle from the car. He was grizzling so I gave him the keys to hold — they always keep him quiet — and just as we got here he threw them away. I didn't see, but I think they must have gone down that drain. I've looked everywhere!"

It was an exclamation of frustration, a frustration aggravated by the cries of the cross child.

"Let me help you."

Together they hunted up and down the flowerbed, parting the scented leaves and peering into the bottomless drain. The search was fruitless.

"I'll have to go home and get my spare keys."

"Do you live far away? I can drive you."

"Oh no, that would be too much trouble." She was not used to accepting help from strangers and found it hard to be gracious. "I can take a taxi. I wouldn't dream of it."

"Nonsense! Is it far?"

"Only a little way. It's almost near enough to walk, but that'd take too long." She wavered; it would be so easy.

"Well, that's simple. We'll put the stroller in the boot."

In the car the baby, held in his mother's arms, was pacified for the moment and, as they drove, the mother talked about herself in a nervous rush, as if she were anxious to establish her credentials in order to justify herself for allowing someone she had never met assist her, which was for her so unusual.

"I always go to lunch with my mother on Wednesdays, after I've been to the hospital. It's my husband's golf day. The firm likes him to go to the club, he makes contacts there. He's very good, very thoughtful. He always rings me at Mum's to make sure I'm all right. It's too early yet" — she glanced at a tiny silver watch set in a plaited gold and silver bracelet, a piece of jewellery rather than necessary machinery — "they won't worry about me. The firm's given him a car and I've got a Honda Civic of my own. He's very considerate, he gave me the Honda. Says he can't bear women who sit at home all day, they only get boring. He likes me to go out with my friends. Besides, with the car I can get around when he's away on business. He has to go away a lot these days. He went to the States last year, that's when he bought me the watch, but he always brings me something after a business trip. I like that. Some men don't seem to care at all. I don't know how their wives put up with it. He gave me this ring when the baby was born. It's a sapphire he got in Hong Kong. I love blue stones, and diamonds do set them off."

She held up her hand, turning it this way and that in order to admire her husband's gift. The woman glanced at it briefly, her attention on the road, and thought to herself that the firm must value the up and coming young man highly.

"It's just round the corner on the left, the one with the birch trees in the front garden. We planted those when we first moved there. I love birch trees and white flowers. I only plant white or blue, none of those showy colours like they have at the hospital." She gave a little pout of distaste. As they pulled up, her expression altered to one of puzzlement.

"That's funny, there's my husband's car in the drive, the grey Commodore. He usually goes straight to golf from the office. Do come in while I find the keys."

The front door was white-painted wood, panelled in squares and ornamented with a brass knocker and doorknob. The young woman turned the key.

"Hullo, it's me," she called as she pushed open the door.

As the door opened the woman behind her glimpsed a man in the middle of the hall, his back towards them. He swung round, his startlement clear on his face.

"Darling, whatever are you doing home? You'll never guess what happened."

At that moment a voice from somewhere at the back of the house called in a clear soprano.

"Darls, I can't find the lemons — where have you hidden them, you wicked man? I want my gin and tonic. I need a quick one quickly."

Standing at the entrance, the woman saw a figure wearing a low-cut floral sundress, which set off her plump shoulders and generously displayed the globes of her breasts, emerge into the hall. Her big eyes were made bigger with dark eye shadow, and in one hand she held a gin bottle.

"Do you want —?" she began.

There was a total hush. All four froze and stood staring at each other. For several seconds no one moved, no one had a word to say. Then the baby gave a loud scream.

"Take him." His mother shoved the baby at his father, her voice blurred. "I'll get his bottle. I came for my spare keys."

Two minutes later she returned, carrying a basket and dropping the keys into it beside the bottle.

"Give him to me." The skin of her face and lips was taut.

The woman helped her into the car. As they drove back to the hospital the baby's yells precluded any conversation. In the carpark he quietened when they put him in his stroller.

The young woman stood quite still and silent for a minute, looking into the distance, while the woman, distressed, watched her.

"The bastard, the lousy bastard," she finally uttered in a voice of sharp steel. "I've always played fair with him, even when he's been away. I've had plenty of opportunities. And I keep myself nice."

She glanced down at her trim figure with a look of purely sexual appraisal.

"How could he? He's disgusting, filthy. I'll never let him touch me again. Never. I couldn't bear it. Why did he do it, why? To think I've played fair all this time. Did you see her, did you just see?"

Now her tongue had broken loose there was no stopping it. For a short time the woman allowed her this relief. Then she intervened.

"I don't think you should drive yourself just now. I'll drive you to your mother's," she said firmly.

The years of authority in her voice had their effect, and the young woman seemed about to acquiesce.

"Do you have to see your friend upstairs first?"

"My friend. That's funny. My friend is *his* mother. She's a heart patient and he makes me go and visit her every week before I see my own mother. She's been in hospital for months. He doesn't like hospital visiting. It makes him feel sick. It makes me feel sick too. I hate hospitals."

"You take the baby. I'll take the basket."

At that moment a grey car swung into the carpark and screeched to a halt in front of them. Out of it jumped the man. There was no sign of guilt in his expression. He was the aggressive male, all-conquering, and the woman could smell his sweat as he marched towards his wife and grabbed her arm.

"Get your hands off me."

She turned her head and refused to look at him.

"I will not. You come home with me right now and we'll talk there."

She withstood him furiously, isolated and hard in her anger, a stone figure of rage and desolation. Planting himself in front of her, he stood daring her to defy him, to pit her will against his dominating masculinity. She would not look into his eyes, but gazed coldly at some far tree.

Suddenly she swung round, tossed back her hair and, raising her chin, flung her own challenge at him with a look. Now it was she who dared him. With a half smile on her face she walked towards his car.

"You can get my car home somehow." She thrust the baby onto the front scat, next to her basket.

The woman watched them go. On an impulse she went up to her son's ward and, unnoticed by him, stood at the door and watched him for some time. She needed to see someone of her own family, her own blood and, as she watched him playing happily on the floor with a box of brightly painted blocks, a feeling of tenderness towards him, such as she had not known for a long time, flowed over her. Instead of returning home at once she went to walk for a while in the rose garden. She would have a lot to talk about with her husband tonight.

In the car the man and woman stared straight ahead at the road. Neither noticed that the baby, propped against the basket, had grabbed her spare car keys and dropped them down the crack beside the gear lever.

THE SNAKE

She lay in bed listening to the lions roaring a couple of kilometres away; a rough sound, a bracket of panting coughs in the midnight silence. To her it was a homely noise, one of the sounds she had grown up with in the city — the roaring of the lions in the zoo, and the rhythmic clack and clatter of train wheels running along the river valley and disappearing into the night and the far north.

The lions ceased their grumbling and she was falling back to sleep when she suddenly remembered the snake under her bed and was wide awake again. She had meant to remove it before she went to bed, but then she had forgotten about it.

A carpet snake, perfectly harmless, it was elegantly marked in brown and ochre diamonds and diagonals, shining now in the beauty of a freshly cast skin. It was safely contained in a travelling box specially designed to give it sufficient air and intended to disguise from nervous fellow passengers that their companion was not the family cat, which they presumably would imagine it to be.

The snake did not belong to her; she was merely acting as a temporary hostess. She had never felt an affinity with snakes and was reluctant to accommodate this one longer than was necessary. She could remember being taken as a child to the Snake Park where she had been photographed with various reptiles draped around her neck. Posing thus had been bravado — she hated the feeling of their movement on her skin — but she had been too obstinate to admit her cowardice.

That morning, so far away now in time and distance, her husband had been angry that she proposed to drive the snake in its box all the way to the city in order to give it to a friend. In his opinion snakes were vermin and keeping one as a pet a townsman's unnatural eccentricity.

They lived on a property in the dry north country where they could carry only one sheep to ten hectares. Mustering was done on motorbikes, which were loaded onto the back of a truck and carried to the farthest corners of the place, away across dim blue lines of hills which barely indented the horizon.

The motorbikes meant that the men could do a day's work and be back at the homestead for the evening meal. In the late afternoon sunlight she would watch for the plume of dust which flew liked a pennant behind the approaching truck and told her that it was time to put dinner in the oven. She seldom had to spend a night alone.

She would hear the voices of the men calling to each other in the yard as they dispersed for the night, then the hollow tramp of her husband's feet on the wooden steps leading up to the verandah. He never came to greet her until he had showered in the bathroom which opened off the end of the verandah. There she left his clean clothes every afternoon, a sharply pressed blue shirt and white cotton trousers.

She would put the last touches to the dinner in the kitchen, waiting for him to come in with his usual greeting.

"Hello, angel, how's my girl?"

Then, while they sat together with a drink for half an hour, peacefully letting the sun go down, he would tell her all the station news. After dinner he would go to his office to deal with the paperwork which piled up there; she would take up one of the books which came in the mail from the library every month.

Her days were overflowingly busy, with her work in the house and about the place, the radio 'sked', the mail to attend to. In the afternoons she liked to spend some time in her patch of garden. There was enough water to support a square of lawn in front of the house and a few flowers — pink impatiens, some succulents — below the verandah, and there were citrus trees against the fence. Sometimes she went beyond the garden fence and stood on a rocky knoll beneath a she-oak. The least breeze made a susurration in the long tresses of foliage. On certain days she could see from there the neighbours' house, forty kilometres away, reflected in a mirage on the horizon. She could even see a tractor driving from the shed. She would return to her own empty house entertained by that strange vision in the sky.

They had little in common with their neighbours. The wife was a stringy little woman with a fawn neck and fawn hair, who resented the sugar ants which invaded her cupboards, the dirt on her husband's boots and a great many other things about her life, and whose only enjoyment was an opportunity to complain about them. Her husband was a silent, hard-working man who resented his wife. They had a son, Gus, an unattractive young man of limited abilities and thick lips on whom his mother doted. His great pleasure in life was his collection of lizards which lived in a variety of boxes in his bedroom, a fibro-lined tin shed near the chook yard. He crooned and pored over his treasured pets every evening before he went to bed. He also had one end of the yard wired as an aviary, where he kept parrots: these he was adept at catching in the trees along the dry watercourses. His closest friend was a cockatoo which shrieked "Night-night cocky, fuck off" to anyone who would listen.

The two neighbours prided themselves on being self-sufficient, but each family turned to the other in an emergency and there was an unexpected bond between them.

It had been due to Gus that their only child, a daughter called Joanna, was almost killed in an accident some years before. She was eighteen at the time and had just left school. On the first night of her holidays she came into the kitchen where her mother was peeling potatoes and settled happily into a chair at the table.

"It's just wonderful to be back," she said and, jumping up, gave her mother a huge hug. "Look what I brought you — a bag of gooseberries."

"That's a real treat. I'll make gooseberry fool."

"I'll top and tail them." Joanna chose a sharp knife. "I can't wait to go round the place with Dad."

"He's been working on the second motorbike for you. There was some dirt in the carburettor."

Joanna was a keen bike rider, as skilled as any of the men. All that summer she worked beside her father whenever possible. It was a particularly long hot season, but at the end of it came a week of overcast skies. Joanna and her father were riding back one evening after checking a windmill. There was a speckle of rain and a nagging wind that stirred up whorls of red dust. They were approaching a dry watercourse where there was a permanent spring-fed pool which attracted a number of birds. It was a favourite place of Joanna's and she made a quick spurt ahead on the bike, eager to see the birds gathered for their evening drink. As she shot up over the steep sandy bank she saw a battered utility parked right in the centre of the track. She had barely time to slew the bike sideways and it clipped the corner of the tray. Joanna flew three metres through the air and landed heavily on her back, one leg doubled up beneath her and the bike on top of her, churning the sand.

A quarter of an hour later Gus was knocking on the back door of the house.

"Missus," he called, "Missus. Something's happened. The boss says bring a mattress and blankets in the back of the ute. I was only watching them birds too."

So did the mother learn of Joanna's accident.

Her leg was badly broken and needed many months of treatment in hospital. At that time they bought the little city house from where the lions could be heard in the dead of night, so that the mother could be near Joanna and care for her at home on those occasions when she was allowed to leave the hospital briefly. Mother and daughter had always been close and the bond between them strengthened under these difficulties. They were devoted companions and even at the worst times managed to find some amusement in their distress. But the woman missed her husband grievously and longed for his warmth and her busy station days, though she managed to keep her miseries to herself.

The small blue-stone house was an exact replica of several others in the street. Numbers 12, 14, 16 and 18 were all alike, wide enough only for one room and a long corridor into which the rooms opened. A tiny garden the width of one pace separated the street from the narrow verandahs. The only exterior differences lay in the colours the occupants chose to paint their front doors, their fences and whether or not they were conscientious gardeners. Her own garden was overgrown due to recent neglect and the front room was darkened by trails of creeper hanging from the verandah. The solid little houses, only about twenty of them in the short, tucked-away street, had been built for artisans a hundred years ago. Since then the street had come up in the world a little, but not too much, and the inhabitants were remarkably anonymous. Such were their differing interests that they sometimes went for weeks without speaking to each other.

At the time when Joanna was in hospital, the countrywoman made a new friend. It was on a day in early spring when the urgent sunshine drew her outside; she needed to work in the garden to strengthen her spirit. She was kneeling in the tiny strip of front garden, contentedly pulling out soursobs and enjoying the warm air, when she looked up and saw an eye gazing at her and then two eyes, through a chink in the brush fence. The eyes were dark and set in a head which was at that moment twisted sideways to make the best use of the aperture.

"Hullo," said a voice. "Can I come in?"

Surprised, she replied, "Yes, I suppose so," and leant back on her heels.

A very small boy, barefoot and wearing a grubby T-shirt, clicked open the gate and walked in, clutching a loaf of bread to his chest like a teddy bear.

"Hullo," he said again. "Can I talk to you?"

Without fuss he settled himself on a stool which stood on the verandah. Such aplomb in so young a child was almost alarming. He was dark with the kind of well-formed good looks which betokened something noble in his ancestry, the woman thought romantically.

"What's your name?" he asked.

"Phillida," she replied.

"That's not a real name. No one at school is called Phillida. I'll call you Mrs Phil."

She could think of no comment and laughed. "Are you old enough to go to school?"

"Of course, I was June intake. It's the only time I'll be the same number as my brothers."

"What do you mean?"

"I'm five, coming six, and I've got five brothers."

"Are you the youngest?"

"Yes. My oldest brother's my best brother."

"Why's that?"

"He's grown-up and he brings me things."

"What sort of things?"

"Lizards and once a pair of budgies. I've got them in a cage. When I'm big I'm going to have a snake."

"Goodness, what sort of snake?"

"A python! My brother says they won't hurt you. They keep down the mice."

"I know someone in the country who keeps lizards and birds. How strange."

"What sort? How many?"

"I'm not too sure — I don't know him very well. Shouldn't you be at home? Your mother might worry."

"She won't mind, she's busy. She's a dressmaker and she's finishing a wedding dress today. She always lets me buy the bread."

"Anyway, perhaps you'd better go back now."

"All right, but I'll come again." He slipped off the stool and pattered quietly out the gate, leaving Phillida amused and touched by his friendliness. She had forgotten to ask his name.

The next day she was removing a tray of rock buns from the oven when she looked down the corridor and saw that he was standing at the front door.

"Can I come in?" he called.

"I expect so." She was startled again.

He joined her in the kitchen and gazed fascinated at the spicy hot rock buns, as though every one of his senses were taking them in. But he was not as crass as to ask directly for one.

She offered him the tray. "Don't burn your tongue, they're still hot. You didn't tell me your name yesterday."

"It's Paul."

He sat down at the table and, with a discerning hand, chose a bun on the side farthest from him. By the time they had finished talking he had eaten half the trayful.

Again Phillida said:

"I think you should go home. I'll walk back with you." She had decided she ought to speak to his mother.

"It's that house on the corner."

The front door of the house gave directly onto the street and, Paul explained, was always kept locked. When they reached it he bent down to the slit of the letterbox and, lifting the flap with one finger, put his lips to the opening.

"Hey, Mum," he called.

After a few moments the door was opened a short distance by a dark little woman, of clearly the same build as the boy. A gush of stale air poured into the street, smelling of damp towels, wet blankets and sweet talc powder. Seeing the two of them she opened the door a little wider.

"I walked back with Paul," the countrywoman explained. "He came to visit me and I thought you might be worried."

"Oh, he always comes back. He talks to everybody," his mother replied and ran her hand over his hair. "You're a friendly little chap, aren't you?'' She seemed to imply that this was a quality which he had developed for himself, despite her own careful training in suspicion. She laughed. ''You know the whole street, don't you? Will you come in?'' The invitation was reluctantly offered, and Phillida could see that the front room was not only living room and workroom, but a bedroom as well for some of the children.

''Not today, thank you,'' she answered. The little woman had an overeager jauntiness about her, accompanied by an air of self-deprecatory humility, which was in some way repellent. The countrywoman longed to escape from the foetid atmosphere. It seemed the wrong background for Paul. However, he waved one hand cheerfully at her and disappeared inside, while she returned to her own house. Later she learnt that the family's name was Smith.

After that, if she was not at the hospital, he came to see her nearly every day on his way home from school. She was glad of the company and enjoyed talking to this small person. She looked forward to hearing his news and usually made him a cake or biscuits to ease the hunger which smote him about that time of the afternoon. Then she would send him firmly back to his mother, but they were both refreshed by these interchanges.

As the summer came on Joanna finished her treatment and her leg was nearly mended. There was not even a limp and she was ready to go home to the station. They travelled back a few weeks before Christmas, and it was a long time before Phillida returned to the house or saw Paul again.

Over the next few years, Joanna lived in the house while she went to teachers' training college. Her parents came to town to stay with her sometimes, but her father was always worried away from the station and returned as soon as possible. Occasionally Phillida saw Paul, but there was little opportunity to carry on their friendship.

Suddenly and unexpectedly, at the end of the summer vacation, Joanna decided to get married. A young man on a motorbike had appeared at the back door of the homestead one day. He came all the way from Western Australia and was working his way round the country. Phillida's husband had no work to offer, but he took a liking to the young man as they sat drinking tea at the kitchen table.

''My neighbour's putting up a new shed. He came over to

borrow some tools the other day and said he wished he had another pair of hands — you might try there."

The young man, John, called on the neighbours and was taken on at once. Finding the company of his employers uncongenial and Gus's eager leering unattractive, he was happy to ride the forty kilometres to the next homestead as often as possible. He and Joanna were immediately drawn to each other and by the end of summer had fallen in love. They decided to marry.

Phillida thought woefully that their neighbours were making a habit of being involved with major events in their lives.

"You're much too young and Western Australia's much too far," she wailed, pretending despair.

"Oh, Mum, I'm not. Besides, I'll have lots of babies and you can come and look after them."

This seemed a rather arduous and distant compensation, but Phillida prepared herself for the parting with good grace. If Joanna was happy, she was happy also. Nevertheless, after the wedding she felt overwhelmingly bereft. She missed Joanna more than she had thought possible.

To divert herself she decided to go to town, to do up the house which was looking shabby, and see a few friends. It was at this time that she renewed her friendship with Paul.

He had now grown tall enough to see over the fence, and his good looks had increased with his height. She was again cooking rock buns — perhaps the scent had attracted him — when she heard a voice from the front door.

"Can I come in?" And he settled himself at the kitchen table as easily as though he had been doing it every day since they first met. Again he came each afternoon, and she taught him to play backgammon and he taught her card games.

He was still devoted to his increasingly large collection of lizards, birds, white mice and guineapigs. His small backyard was agitated with bird chattering. He still talked of the snake he would have one day; it was the height of his ambition.

One afternoon he arrived triumphant.

"Terry came last night," he announced. Terry was his eldest, his best brother. "Look what he brought me!"

He put his hand into the satchel he was carrying and drew out a small yellow and black lizard, covered from nose to tail with wicked-looking spines which gave him a ferociously cheeky appearance.

"A spiny devil," he said proudly. "Look, the spines are really soft." He fingered one. "Isn't he beautiful?"

Phillida had seen such lizards before and admired it to Paul's satisfaction. "Did you know that his other name is *Moloch horridus*?" she asked.

"No, but I like that. I'll call him Moloch."

Paul often brought Moloch to see her after school; the lizard would sway slightly at the end of the kitchen table, staring at them as they talked, but made no attempt to escape. These times were valuable for Paul; for him it was unusual to talk to an older person on equal terms. In his noisy household there was no place for quiet confidences, whereas Mrs Phil would happily listen to all his stories and comments on the world around him, while they drank cups of tea together. He described to her the escapades of his jovial, bullying brothers with a kind of laughing pride and a detached maturity, as if he clearly understood that he was different from them. He hero-worshipped Terry, for no very good reason, she sometimes thought, and often mentioned his exploits. He was working up north somewhere and only infrequently sent his mum a postcard. Paul seemed vague as to what he did or where he was exactly. Sometimes Terry appeared briefly for a night, as he had recently done, and went away again as quickly.

Paul was no longer happy at school. One of the schoolmasters picked on him constantly and contrived to set some of the other children against him. His animals were only partly a compensation for a life that was becoming increasingly solitary. Phillida could picture the situation easily. That air of aristocratic self-possession, which she had noticed about him from the beginning, had increased as he grew older. She imagined how a small-minded teacher might resent this, suspecting impertinence and mockery behind the boy's clear, cool look. Unnecessarily, she thought, for Paul had an exceptionally sweet nature and was ready to accept the world for what it was, and schoolteachers as an ordained part of that world. He bore no resentment and was bewildered by the petty nastiness which he was made to suffer. From what Paul told her, the countrywoman could see that the master jeered obliquely even at his best efforts; the boy's only defence was a withdrawing into himself which irked the other children.

"Here comes Liz-o," they taunted him. "Bats in his belfry and lizards for his lunch."

It became a chant in the playground, and no one tried to check it. One or two of the boys stood up for him, which made his life tolerable, but he was learning more about cruelty than he could express in words.

Phillida ached to help him. Her affection for him deepened each day, and the boy was equally devoted to her. His visits to her were always special occasions, and he had the relief of pouring out his feelings in a way he could never do at home. So she yearned after him almost as she would have done over one of her own family. She once asked his mother if he could spend some of his holidays in the country with her. Mrs Smith was clearly horrified.

"Oh", she said. "He's never been away from home. I don't think he'd like that at all. So far away."

Phillida was not so certain, but the idea obviously alarmed his mother so much that she did not press the matter. Instead, she tried to tell him something about her life in the country, a life which was almost incomprehensible to him.

"I can't buy a packet of needles without writing a letter," she once told him.

This was amazing to one whose whole existence depended on constant visits to the corner store. He questioned her about every detail. In particular he often asked about Gus and his birds and lizards. A kindred spirit, he obviously thought.

"That friend of yours — how many parrots has he got?"

She could not convey any idea of distance to him at all, or make him understand that she seldom visited the neighbours.

"He's not exactly a friend," she said. "I've never seen his parrots, but he always seems to be hanging around our place looking for more." She disapproved of anyone catching wild birds and her husband had more than once sent Gus on his way. She felt differently about birds bred in captivity.

"What about the bikes? Could I ride one?" She knew more about these than captive wildlife.

The renovations to the house were finished, but she stayed on. She knew that her presence in the street was a help to Paul and could hardly bring herself to leave. But one day her husband rang her from the nearest town where he had gone on a stores run, and the sound of his voice made her long to be with him. She could hear his loneliness on the telephone.

She hastily appointed Paul her official gardener so that he

could do the watering. He was big enough now for such responsibilities, and the thought of the money she would pay him cheered him, despite having to say goodbye.

Quickly she packed up and returned home.

"I don't think I could bear you to be away again for so long," her husband said as he held her closely.

Happy again in her own place, it was months before she even thought of going to the city. Then, during the school holidays, she had a rush of visitors all excited by the beauty of the country and longing to be shown the cliffs and caves in the gorges behind the homestead. They were not close friends and, meaning well, they sympathised with her in her lonely life, a sympathy to which she did not take kindly. She thought to herself tartly:

"Every time anyone comes here for any reason at all, I have to put them up, and there's always someone extra for a meal. I could do with a bit of peace now and then."

Thinking that she was weary and growing bad-tempered, she decided on a quick shopping expedition to town.

"Only four or five days," she promised her husband.

She went to the implement shed where one of the men was welding a split in the muffler of her car. The shed was a dark cavern and the only light the constellation of sparks from the welder in the far corner. As she waited to speak, she suddenly realised that Gus was standing in the shadows, almost invisible.

"Good gracious, Gus, what are you doing here?"

Gus giggled, as he often did.

"I come to get me snake," he said.

"What snake?"

"Chap left him for me." He indicated a box, beautifully crafted by a careful bushman with all the time in the world to finish each detail to perfection.

She peered at the box. "Isn't it dangerous?"

"No, it's a carpet snake." He opened the lid and in the dark interior she could faintly see the coiled form.

Suddenly she thought of Paul. Here was the thing he had always wanted more than anything in the world. Perhaps it would help him over his difficult times if she gave it to him.

"Would you sell it to me, Gus? I'm going to the city tomorrow, and a friend of mine there has always wanted a snake."

"To the city." His mouth hung open loosely, and he giggled again. "I never been to the city. I'm going there one day. Friend of mine says he'll show me round if I give him some of me birds. Reckons there's a zoo there with parrots as big as wedgies, all colours, all from some place in America." In the shadows she saw his leer of anticipation.

"Would you sell the snake to me?"

"Dunno, I suppose I might." Gus had little need for money except on his occasional expeditions to the nearest country town 100 kilometres away, but for a visit to the city — perhaps he might need some cash. The deal was struck.

Gus carried the box from the darkness into the bright sunlight and set it on a corner of the verandah.

"What do I have to do for it?" she asked with a small shudder of distaste.

"Oh nothing, missus. He only needs feeding every couple of days, a mouse or something. If your friend knows, he'll be right."

So the snake became her responsibility and the cause of one of her infrequent arguments with her husband.

As soon as she reached town she set out to find Paul, even though the afternoon was drawing in and a light rain was falling. She needed exercise after her drive and was glad of the walk up the street. She rattled the tinny little knocker on his front door and waited a long time before footsteps approached. She heard a bolt being drawn; the doorknob turned and Mrs Smith opened the door a few inches, sufficiently for the musty air inside to gush out and its odour to flow about her. Though the dressmaker was usually overeffusive whenever she saw her, today she was obviously not in the mood for friendly exchanges. She stood wordless for a minute and then greeted her curtly.

"I've just arrived and I've got something for Paul. Is he home?"

"No."

"Do you know when he'll be back?"

"No."

"Could you ask him to come and see me when he gets home?"

"All right, but he might be too late tonight."

There was clearly no more to be said so, uttering a few amiabilities for form's sake, she left and turned back to her own house. She was suddenly flattened with disappointment. She had been thinking of the moment all day, with rising excitement. This present was for her more than a gift; it was a proof that she could bring something from her own life to help Paul.

It had not occurred to her that he might not be there to greet her immediately she arrived, and she felt as disappointed as if she had stepped off an aircraft and found no one there to meet her. She had been allowing herself the luxury of pouring out her affection unchecked, and now it must be held back. Nor had it occurred to her that the snake might not be welcome in the Smith household. She told herself that she was being ridiculously sensitive about the boy's absence, and lifted her head higher to the gentle rain. It was almost dark.

A familiar figure suddenly appeared beside her out of the mist. This was old Alice, who lived all alone and who cared nothing for the weather or for the time of day. Always wearing a man's old brown raincoat, she trundled a decrepit pram in which she carried her belongings up and down the streets at all hours. She seemed oblivious of whether the sun was up or the moon and apparently slept just when she felt the need.

"Lovely bit of rain, dear. I like to feel it on me face. Does you good after that dry spell. I'll be out there with me hands in the earth tomorrow. I knew it was coming last week. Me toes began to ache, but I rubbed them with mentholene. You can't beat it."

A faint menthol scent still hung about her.

"Haven't seen you for months, dear. You down for long? I noticed those pot-plants of yours were looking a bit under the weather, so I took them home. It's no use trying pot-plants when you're not there all the time. They're coming on real well now. Well, better be on me way, I suppose, me little dog's waiting for his dinner." She disappeared down the street as Phillida, fuming with resentment as she always did at Alice's depredations, let herself into her house.

She glared at the snake box where she had left it in the hall.

"Blasted snake," she thought, suddenly blaming the creature for everything, and shoved the box out of sight under the bed. It seemed a good place for it. She would move it before she went to bed; she did not like the idea of sleeping with it so near. She set about unpacking, still thinking of Alice.

Alice's chosen profession was picking and stealing, though she preferred to call it charitable work for the reason that when she grew tired of one of her acquisitions, she would bestow it on someone whom she considered less fortunate than herself. She looked after her neighbours in her own fashion and knew their business as well as they did themselves. She was interested in everyone.

Alice was an expert in her field and proud of her expertise, about which she liked to boast rather than attempt to disguise. Goldfish in particular she could never resist, and she had a pond in her backyard bountifully stocked with the most elegant and lacy-finned fish, culled from grander neighbourhood pools. She carried for the purpose in the bottom of her pram a little net which she had made from an ancient piece of hat-veiling. She demonstrated the net to chosen friends and once produced it to show "that nice girl from the country". Phillida knew from experience that it was no use protesting and could not help laughing at Alice's brazen ingenuousness.

"Do you really think you should?" was all she allowed herself to say.

"Oh, yes, dear, it's quite all right. I just pop in to keep an eye on things when I know they're away. They'd be glad for me to have something for me pains."

Alice's activities extended to anything which was left lying about. This included the wooden stool on the countrywoman's front verandah on which Paul had first perched himself. As she had not seen Alice load it onto her pram, she could not bring herself to accuse the old woman of theft, but she took care after that to carry her possessions inside. She had been rather fond of that stool.

Alice lived well. She always knew when to be in the right place at the right time. When the greengrocer closed his shop for the weekend, she would stand with her pram near his shutters and usually profited. She found herself frequently at the butcher's back door when he was disposing of unwanted offal. There were often good bones with enough meat on them to be worth carrying home. Her favourite dish was boiled marrow bones. Her little dog lived on the scraps.

Paul did not come that evening, which did not surprise Phillida on such a night. After a meal she recovered her spirits and went to bed early, full of cheerful plans for the next day.

Now, an hour or two later she had stirred. The thought of the snake wakened her thoroughly; she disliked having it in her bedroom. Dragging the box from under the bed and pleased to see that the catch was still safely fast, she put it in the hall to be rid of it.

She went to the window and stared out. The sky glowed copper from the reflection of the city lights, and small yellow clouds hung above the rooftops. How strange it was that it was never completely dark in town. Only the brightest stars showed beyond the metallic screen of light. Yet it was often more silent in this quiet street than ever it was in the country. From her bed at home she could always hear the sounds of grazing stock or of insects and eerie night birds. Here, at this moment, there was a total absence of sound, until, far away, the siren of an ambulance wailed. Her heart went out to some poor soul, lonely and suffering at this unsympathetic hour.

She looked across the narrow path which separated her house from the next one. She knew the house was empty; the last owners had left some time ago. While they had lived there she had tried to be friendly, but her cheerful greetings in the street had been snubbed, and any neighbourly gestures haughtily refused. So she gave up her effort. In the city it was possible to ignore one's neighbours with impunity. She had heard the man and the woman quarrelling bitterly late one night. After that the husband had disappeared, and it was rumoured at the corner deli that he had thrown himself under a train. But no one knew for certain, so encapsulated were their lives. All she could see from where she stood now were two blank windows, bare of curtains.

She shivered. The contented mood which had led her back to her girlhood memories of the lions roaring had passed with the sound of the ambulance, and now she felt that there was something sinister in the air. Born a city girl, she was not usually nervous about spending a few nights alone. She enjoyed the novelty of solitude and independence. Life in the country had been quite foreign to her when she first married, but now she was as much a part of it as a lizard standing on a rock, and felt like a stranger in her own birthplace.

Nevertheless, she loved this shabby stone house and enjoyed her excursions to town. Standing at the window and watching the yellow clouds form and re-form above the houses, she thought of the life going on in the street around her, so much of it hidden and unknown. How mysterious it was. The activities within each little house might never impinge on those of the ones beside it if the people living there chose to remain private and solitary. How little she knew of all those men and women sleeping within a few hundred metres of where she stood. Two doors away lived a young couple with a baby. He left early for work every morning in a neat suit, dark with a dark tie, and a briefcase. Was the girl lonely at home all day, or was she glad to be rid of him? A retired postmaster and his wife had bought the third house along. How did he pass his time? Perhaps he collected stamps.

Again she shivered. The street, which she usually thought of as being full of warmth and interesting diversity, seemed suddenly heartless and drab. She was really cold now and climbed back into bed.

In the morning she stood at her back door enjoying the early sun shining through the translucent blue flowers of a convolvulus climbing along the fence. She thought again of the snake, but knew she would have to wait until Paul came home from school to give him his present. She hoped that by then his mother would be a little more co-operative.

As the sun was rising above the leaves, she saw Alice pottering along the path next door. She had given up trying to admonish Alice for trespassing and, remembering that she had brought the old woman a dozen eggs from her own hens, took them to her.

"I've just been watering those climbers at the back fence, dear — they needed a good soak. You can't let climbers die just like that. That woman never made her garden look much. She used to drink, you know. She took a knife to *him*. You wouldn't have thought it to see her in the street, all dressed up in that smart suit."

She always knew the details and more of any scandal.

In her hands she carried a bunch of geraniums, obviously just filched from someone's garden. It was impossible to chide her. She followed the countrywoman into her front hall and pointed to the snake box.

"Now there's a nice box. Just the size for a cat or a little dog. Useful."

"Yes, it belongs to a friend of mine," Phillida said quickly.

"I'm just going to take these geraniums to the girl with the baby. She's got a nasty cold. Caught it from the baby. I don't like the sound of his cough either. He's a bad colour. I told her raw scraped steak and cod-liver oil."

She pulled a sprig or two of white jasmine from the creeper on the verandah post and added it to her posy.

"Did you hear about the postmaster? Won a lottery. He wanted to go to the Barrier Reef but his wife didn't feel up to it, so they've taken a house at the beach for a month instead. I know they'd want me to keep an eye on their garden too. The quinces on their tree are just coming ripe. I love a stewed quince."

There was nothing to be done about her neighbourly attentions.

"Ta-ta, dear. Have a happy day."

The woman did indeed have a happy day, shopping. In the afternoon she returned full of anticipation about seeing Paul, but there was no sign of him. Hurt and puzzled, she worried that for some reason his mother might have forbidden him to come and see her. She had acted to strangely yesterday that she hardly liked to call on her again. She was in a quandary about what best to do and eventually decided to do nothing. Changing her dress, she went to dine with friends and came home rather late. Her friends were concerned about her being alone in the house at night, but since she thought that she possessed nothing worth stealing, and rape was not a matter which entered her consideration, she was less nervous than they were. However, they harped on the question so much during the evening, citing so many examples of lone women being assaulted in various unpleasant ways that she realised, as she drove back to the house through a gloomy drizzle, that she was feeling edgy. She was annoyed with herself for what she judged a feeble spirit.

Rebuking herself for silly qualms, she pulled up at her front gate and gave a great start of fright as she did so. As if the very embodiment of her fears was waiting for her, she could see the figure of a man half-hidden behind the tangled jasmine. He was peering through the front window, and did not move at her approach. He was short and heavily built, wearing a black leather jacket.

Leaving the car engine running, she wound down the window and called:

"Are you looking for someone?"

He swung around and stepped out from behind the sheltering foliage and, though it was hard to see his face clearly in the dim streetlight, she had the impression of something smooth and pallid, like a polished rock, with a high dome of forehead across which soft hair was scraped. He might have been in his twenties. There was a gleam of solid white teeth, a long smile which made him seem more menacing, and he replied softly:

"No, I think this is the wrong house."

Even then he hardly moved and she could feel her fright increasing as she held the car wheel tightly. She was almost ready to accelerate away when he turned and walked quickly off into the rain. Relieved but shaken, she had difficulty in putting her latch key in the lock.

Inside the house it was so still and safe that she decided that her feeling of alarm had been ridiculously exaggerated, and she soon felt perfectly calm again. She gave the episode a quick thought in the shower next morning, but viewed it as something which would make an entertaining anecdote at dinner, casting herself as the poor little woman who saw threats behind every post.

A little later Alice came past on her early round. Phillida was enjoying the luxury of the morning paper and coffee when she heard Alice calling from the front door. Rather resentfully, she felt obliged to pour her a cup. Alice opened the neck of her raincoat and fanned herself with the lapels.

"I feel all hot. Those Smith kids on the corner give me that much cheek. There were two of them up a tree this morning. They threw rotten plums in my pram, dirty little buggers. It wouldn't hurt their dad to give those kids a belting, but he's not around half the time. I don't go much on their mum either, mingy little woman — wouldn't give you an old newspaper."

"She's a good dressmaker," the woman said peaceably. She was tired of Alice's gossip and wished she would go away.

"I wouldn't trust her. She's all over you like a rash one minute, and the next thing you'd think she'd slap your face."

Phillida knew what she meant. Alice continued relentlessly.

"I never knew what happened to that eldest boy of hers either, and she's not telling."

"I suppose that's up to her. I don't know the elder ones. Paul's my particular friend. He's a great help to me in the garden."

"Yes, well . . . I must be off. You got any empty bottles? Nice box, that," and she pointed again to the snake box.

Phillida did not answer, but she was beginning to worry that the snake might soon be needing nourishment. Besides, she could hardly wait to see Paul's face when he opened the box.

She spent the day with an old school friend who was also Joanna's godmother, and intended to be back in good time to find Paul. She did not confide in her friend the saga of the snake, nor her feelings for the child. They were something precious, for her alone.

Just as she was about to leave, there was a phone-call to say that one of her friend's children had fallen out of a tree he had been climbing at school. The boy had broken his arm and there seemed nothing for Phillida to do but stay and mind the other children while his mother took him to the hospital. She had so often helped Phillida when Joanna was ill. So Phillida was again late returning to her house. Not until she turned into the street did she remember her visitor of the night before, and she glanced warily in every direction to make sure that he was not there. All was safe and quiet. She could hear the lions roaring as she hung up her coat in the silent bedroom. She turned out the lights and went to make sure that the back door was locked. As she did so she glanced into the little garden.

Under the shadow of a loquat tree in the corner stood the man in the dark jacket.

She almost cried out, but managed to stifle her exclamation and, holding her hand to her throat, watched him cautiously for some time. He could not see her from where he stood. The disguise of darkness gave her a certain feeling of safety, but the menace of the stocky figure so close to her made her breath come in short gasps.

She struggled to be calm and to observe his movements. What was he after? Why had he come a second time? If he was waiting for her, what was he going to do next? He showed no sign of moving nor of coming towards the door. She needed help badly, but hardly dared move in case he saw her. She must reach the telephone, though she dreaded the sound of her voice. At last she forced herself to move and ring the police.

Her action gave her courage. She was not given to hysterics and was perfectly composed by the time two awkward young policemen, a pair of nice shy lads, came to the door. They dutifully searched the garden, but found no sign of the intruder and could not account for whence he had come or how. They clearly had no more idea of what to do about the affair than they knew what to do with their hats in the house. These they kept tucking under their arms as they promised they would watch the house that night.

"Doubt he'll trouble you again. He would've heard us. Anyway, we'll report it."

Reassured, she said goodnight and let them out the door.

The next day she considered her position. Twice she had been troubled by the strange man. Was it sensible to stay in the house alone? Both pride and obstinacy forbade her to go away. She valued her ability to look after herself. Besides, she told herself in the bravery of early morning light, she was not really frightened. The locks on the doors were secure, the windows barred. So she persuaded herself.

The day was soft and balmy and in the afternoon she decided to visit the zoo. She was worried about the snake and decided to ask one of the keepers for advice about its care and feeding. The zoo was a favourite place of hers; she had brought Paul here several times. The reptile house was the chief attraction, and he would stand absorbed in watching the reptiles' forms for so long that she would grow bored and stroll outside to wait for him in the sun. She preferred the lions and was delighted when they were lively enough to wrestle and play like kittens. Paul's second love was the parrots, and he knew the geography of the bird cages as well as some children know their own gardens. He even had names for certain parrots.

Today she went directly to the reptile house and enquired about the keeper from a young man gathering up rubbish. The keeper was away having his tea but would be back in half an hour, she was told, so she went to visit the lions to pass the time. She sat down near the cage and for a long time was perfectly contented with their company and her own. The place was peaceful and deserted at this hour of day. Mothers and children had gone home to tea and only a few attendants were about, with their barrows and brooms. The bees droned in a flowering gum above her and she fell half-asleep in the mid-afternoon sun. Thirsty, she made her way to the kiosk, still dreamy with the sun, not quite awake. As she approached the small pavilion she suddenly stopped where she stood. Standing as still as ever, unobtrusive in the shadow of the kiosk verandah, was the man in the leather jacket. The stance, with arms held slightly away from his sides and the pale domed face tilted, was unmistakable. His outline was now very familiar to her. He was looking in another direction and had not noticed her, she felt sure. Her palms sweating, the fear in her chest trying to burst forth, she slipped quickly behind a hedge, hardly knowing what to think or do. It was possible to reach the gate by a sheltered path and this she hurried along in great agitation. It could surely not be a coincidence that the man was at the zoo at the same time as she, yet she was quite certain that he had not seen her approach. She arrived at the little house full of nervous doubts and questions, her self-assurance beginning to leak away.

She was so taken up with her thoughts that, as she parked the car, she did not notice the knots of people in the street. Then, as she stepped onto the verandah, she realised that there was something unusual happening and turned back. Several women were standing in the middle of the road, caught up in animated conversation. A few men, just home from work, were conferring discreetly by a gate.

Mrs Smith, at the centre of a group which crowded close to hear her words, was clearly the source of all this unusual activity and obviously overwrought. She approached Phillida, feverishly apologetic for herself, distraught and yet subdued.

"It's my Paul," she said indistinctly. "He's disappeared. He said he'd run away one day and I never took any notice and now he's gone."

Phillida drew in her breath.

"Gone where?" she cried out in distress.

"I don't know — all I know is it's that teacher, I'm sure." Tears started in her eyes, and she rubbed them away with a grey handkerchief crumpled to a rag.

"He's been so queer, putting his head up in the air the way he does and not talking to anyone."

Phillida could picture that look of Paul's, that look which could very easily be mistaken for arrogance by those who did not know him. If only she could have been there to help him.

"Then he came home one day and flew out at us. Kicked a kitchen chair so that it broke, and yelled and screamed. He said he'd run away and he wouldn't go back to school. Then he just got quieter and quieter every day."

The tears poured out now and the grey rag was sodden.

Phillida could have wept herself as she listened to the story. "We knew it was something about the teacher. His Dad was real wild about it."

The father despised schools. He was a fine brawling fellow, who loved his children when he had time, but left his wife to bring them up. He had sent his wife to talk to the teacher, but that had made matters worse. Paul had apparently come home one afternoon more upset than ever. His brothers scorning tears, he had shut himself in the lavatory and his mother thought that he had been crying.

And then he was gone.

"And he took his white mice with him." This was almost too much for his mother; she gave a little sick cry and then tried to hold it back with one hand to her mouth.

"Three days ago he went."

"Three days!" Phillida pictured a multitude of horrifying possibilities at once. "Have you been to the police? What did they say?"

"Oh no, no, no, I can't do that. His dad's away up at Broken Hill after a job. He'd kill me if I went to the police."

The countrywoman felt helpless. Appalled, she could hardly bring herself to face what might have happened. Then she remembered her recent intruder. All her affection for the boy was stirred and she anxiously searched her mind for the best action to take.

"Please, you must go to the police. He may be in danger." She was torn between warning the dressmaker and not wanting to distress her unnecessarily.

The little woman was adamant, her pride rising with difficulty above her self-deprecation.

"I can't give him a police record." She was quite clear about what she thought right. "At first I didn't tell anyone. I thought he'd come back when he got hungry. Then I thought I'd better ask down the street."

Most of the residents of the street were gathered round them now, muttering comments and offering advice. Mrs Smith, though so self-effacing and frightened, was yet so determined to manage in her own way that each one hesitated to force help upon her. The women looked beseechingly at their husbands, hoping they would take charge, but none of the men was prepared to interfere in someone else's family life.

Phillida wished for once that Alice was here with one of her panaceas, but she must have wheeled her pram off to find something tasty for her tea. It was a pity. Alice would have been delighted to bestow her wisdom on the dressmaker, thereby putting her under an obligation.

Phillida could hear murmurs about "child molesters" and "I'd string them up" and, to protect Mrs Smith from further alarm, she drew her into her own house. As she led the way to the kitchen to give her a cup of tea, she did not notice that the snake box was missing from the hall.

Mrs Smith, drooping in her chair as though she could no longer hold herself up, sipped the hot tea and gradually took strength. Her bosom began to pout again and her desperate animation took charge.

"I wish now I'd let him come to you that time, I truly do. He thinks the sun shines out of you."

Phillida made a gesture of deprecation. She did not want the boy's mother to resent such affection.

"He's a wonderful boy. I'm very fond of him," she said quietly.

"He's different from the others, that's his trouble. Don't know where he gets it from. Terry's more like his father — Terry was grateful to your husband for getting him the work that time."

"I don't think I knew about that."

"It was one time when you were down here — he did some fencing or something for your next-door neighbour."

"They're quite a long way from us, actually. Their son collects birds and lizards too, you know. Perhaps when we find Paul he could come and stay with us, after all — I could take him to see them."

She was being deliberately matter-of-fact and optimistic.

"Yes, that might be best for him. Get him out of himself."

Phillida knew that she must somehow persuade Mrs Smith to go to the police, but the most she could manage to extract from her was a promise that, if Paul had not returned by morning, they would go to the police station together. Then she walked Mrs Smith back to her own house, wanting to act as a buffer against further neighbourly comments.

The group in the street had gradually broke up into its individual parts, each disappearing behind impregnable doors.

The tenuous bonds of misfortune which had momentarily linked them would never survive the humdrum demands of everyday living, and they might never be so close again.

Everyone now felt a little resentful that they had come forward so willingly. They had been excited and sympathetic, titillated by their brush with potential tragedy, and yet not one of them had been asked to do anything practical. None of the good advice they had proffered had been taken up. The street was disappointed and critical. "That girl from the country" seemed to think she knew best. Very well then, best leave her to it.

Phillida was far from knowing what to do and spent a miserable evening worrying about the boy. She thought she would never sleep, but finally was forced by exhaustion to go to bed. Last thing before bed she stepped outside for a breath of fresh air and noticed a new moon rising in the east. Superstitiously she made a wish on it for the boy. He was all she could think about.

At about the same time Alice chanced to look out her kitchen window and saw the moon delicately riding above her back fence. She started muttering to herself.

"There now, I've seen it through glass. That's going to bring me bad luck, for sure."

Cursing, she turned to the pan of sausages she was frying on the stove. The kitchen was blue with fatty smoke.

"There, what did I just say? I've half burnt them. Never mind, he'll be so hungry he won't notice."

She forked the sausages into a paper bag, burning her fingers as she did so. She licked a splash of fat from her thumb and padded across the kitchen in her old red slippers.

"It's a bad night, all right. Where are those hard-boiled eggs?"

She stowed eggs and sausages, a few elderly pastries and some excellent tomatoes from the postmaster's garden, in her pram.

"Now, where did I put that box? It'll be better for his mice than that thing he's got. A fancy catch it's got all right. Can't get it open myself, but I dare say he'll manage. There, it just fits nicely in that corner. I know she won't mind me borrowing it, don't know what she wanted it for." She looked round for her wispy little white dog. "Come on, you can come too."

Equipped for her evening's work, she trundled off down the street. In the distance she noticed a short solid man in a leather jacket at the far end of the road.

"Now, I wonder who that is. I reckon I've seen him somewhere. He reminds me of someone."

She stopped her pram by a latched gate and wheeled it inside.

Just then Phillida slipped out of bed. Her restless thoughts were keeping her awake. She stood again at the window as she had stood two nights ago. All was quiet outside; no lions roared, no distant siren sounded, the night itself was asleep.

Suddenly a single rising scream from the empty house next door tore through the silence, followed by the sound of a dog barking wildly. She cried out in fright as she glimpsed a figure through the window. Then came another shriek and, without thinking of the consequences, Phillida grabbed her dressing gown and ran to her front door, struggling in awkward haste to unlock it. Down the path to the back of the house she raced, the dog's barking leading her on.

The door stood open and, inside, a candle was burning on an upturned box. Its flame threw two huge dark shadows on the opposite wall. They were the shadows of Alice and Paul, Alice clutching a broken chair as if for protection and making little noises of terror in her throat, Paul squatting, hands on his knees. Both were staring, fascinated, into the far corner; behind them the little dog was dancing and yapping.

In the corner the carpet snake was stretched along the skirting board, its shining skin gleaming in the flickering light, the dark triangle of its head raised up, poised to strike. As Phillida went to speak, the blunt head shot out and the snake grabbed a cowering white mouse with lightning speed.

There was a pause and a small wail from Paul. "*Jesus!*" he said, barely audibly.

Alice dropped the chair and, swooping down, picked up her dog. For a few seconds all was still and silent. Then a draught blew the candle flame and the monstrous shadows moved again up and down the wall. The door opened quickly and a figure slipped quietly inside. It was the man in the leather jacket.

"You little bastard — there you are. I've been watching the wrong house," he said softly.

Phillida stepped instinctively in front of Paul to protect

him, as she would have done with one of her own. One hand flew out to ward off the evil visitor. He stood in the centre of the room, pale face waxy in the candlelight, arms held out like a wrestler's. He smiled his slow, white-toothed smile again and said in his sibilant voice:

"You needn't worry — I won't hurt him. Where have you been, boy? I even went to the zoo to look for you."

At that moment the room was suddenly lit by the blinding glare of a powerful torch. There was a scuffle, shouting, the candle was knocked over and went out, and the man stood handcuffed between two policemen — not the shy youths who had answered her phone-call, but solid angry men.

Screaming, Paul flew at them.

"Don't you touch him — he's my brother! I did it. I did it."

"Shut up, you," his brother said furiously.

"That's enough, mate. We've got enough on your brother to put him back in gaol for years. He's been sending birds, amongst other things, out of the country in suitcases."

"Let him go!" Paul battered the nearest policeman with his fists.

"Now quieten down, or we'll have to take you too!"

Phillida stepped forward and held him tightly to her.

"I'll look after him," she said.

The policeman swung his torch towards her.

At that moment two more men appeared and Phillida cried out again as she saw that they were dragging Gus between them, frightened to tears, his loose mouth working.

"Gus, what on earth — ?"

"He said he'd meet me at a pub near here," and Gus jerked his head towards the street.

"But he never came," he blubbered. "And then these blokes came and said me ute wasn't registered and they took all me birds. They made me come with them and they asked me all sorts of things. I only wanted to do him a favour and he said he'd show me the city and all. They made me tell them all about him, like, and how he said I could stay in this empty house and all. But it's me birds, they've taken me birds away and I don't know if they'll be all right or anything."

Terry suddenly spoke with a kind of authority.

"Let him go — he doesn't know anything about all this."

That much was obvious.

"When you reported that stranger, lady, it was the first clue we had."

She wondered whether Paul would hold that against her for the rest of her life, but he seemed not to understand and her arms tightened around him.

Some time later the room was quiet, the door shut. The comatose snake had been carefully eased into its box by Gus, who was allowed to go home with Phillida for the night.

In her kitchen Alice was making a cup of tea and muttering to herself again.

"I always knew that eldest boy was in trouble. I hope that woman's grateful to me for looking after the little chap. If it hadn't been for me he might have been starving. That teacher, he's the one his mum ought to be after, telling the whole class the brother was a gaolbird. No wonder Paul wanted to run away. Said he'd been camping in the house a couple of days to get out of school. His mum doesn't know where he is half the time!"

The kettle boiled and she filled the pot.

"But that snake. That nearly done for me. I never could stand snakes. Make me sick. And the way it oozed out of that box when Paul opened it. I still don't like to think about it. I always thought that girl from the country was quite nice too. Fancy keeping a thing like that in your house. It's not natural."

She sipped her tea.

"Pity about the white mice, though. They'll be running all over that empty house. Paul'll miss them — I wonder if I could catch a couple for him. I noticed those people had left a nice little table in the corner. I might go back tomorrow and have a look."

She bit into a soggy pastry which she had rescued.

Phillida was heating milk for cocoa in her own kitchen, trying to calm the distraught Paul whose gulping sobs could still not be contained. Gus was already heavily asleep, fully dressed, on her spare bed. She was not yet quite ready to take Paul home.

"Tell me, what did you mean when you said that you did it?"

His head was down and he would not look at her, but suddenly his eyes came up and she could see how desperately he needed to tell her something. There was a pause while he decided to trust her.

"Terry sent me a message with a friend. They put him in gaol for just nothing. He was only selling birds to people who wanted to keep them. Then he was let out and he wanted some money to go away. So he told me to sneak him some parrots from the zoo. He could sell them. He got me once before to do it — he said they were too crowded in those cages anyway. He showed me how — it's easy at night if you're small like me. I said I'd leave them in a box in the yard."

"And did you?"

"Yes, they're still there. I sent him a message. In the shed at the back of Number 12."

"But this is Number 12."

He stared at her, puzzled. Then he understood.

"So it is. I got muddled."

Such is the resilience of small boys that he burst into sudden peals of laughter.

She took him home to his mother.

Tomorrow she would have to deal with Gus and his latest intrusion on her life.

NEIGHBOURS

She was running, running through the pine forest as fast as the obstacles before her would allow. The tall young trees reached out green arms which linked in front of her, so that on every side she was held in an embrace of branches that parted as she pushed through and closed again behind her. Brushes of pine needles, rougher than cats' tongues, chafed her bare arms. Sometimes her foot caught in a hole and she stumbled, twisting an ankle, but always managing to right herself. Rotting branches of gum trees, left from the time when the original scrub was cleared, waited on the ground to trip her up.

Pale delicate grass sprouted through the soft bed of tan pine needles which muffled the sound of her footsteps. Though she was running through the very outskirts of the forest, it was dark where she was, for the trees caught the shadows immediately and held them fast. She could see the flickering brilliance of the sunlight on the track beyond.

She was escorting a mob of sheep, wethers which had been grazing on this land adjoining her own property, along a track which had been bulldozed as a fire break and an access road around the perimeter of the pine plantation. Having brought the sheep about three kilometres along the track, she had another four kilometres or so to travel before they reached the open gate which led onto her land. Sometimes a few sheep, still hidden within the forest, burst from the trees to join their fellows. Looking up an aisle between the pines, she occasionally saw one or two more and had to make a wide detour to drive them towards the road. So this was why she had to run fast to catch up with the flock, then walk at a steady pace in order to keep them moving. Too much commotion and they would break away into the forest.

They pattered along docilely, the sound of their hooves like rain on fallen leaves. Occasionally they baulked at some obstacle, a water splash or a fallen branch. The leaders propped and stamped, casting their heads from side to side and rolling their eyes, their tongues shooting in and out as they cried in bewilderment. At her urging they started on their way again. She made little noise as she went along, having found that she managed better without shouting and clapping.

An old ewe with a grown lamb at foot was causing trouble at the tail of the mob. She had strayed from the neighbour's paddock and now ran backwards and forwards in indecision, calling agitatedly, her lamb trailing behind. The last wethers were half inclined to follow and the woman was forced to step out on the road and drive her on. As she did so, she gazed across the fence at the red-gold vines, their grapes long since picked, stretching across the hillside of her neighbour's land into the distance.

She had known the property, Glenbarr, well as a child, when the grandmother of the present owner used to give her little iced cakes whenever she was taken to tea. The next generation of men grew up difficult and litigious and gradually alienated the whole district. They were seldom seen except when striding scornfully down the main street of the local town or into the bank. The loss of her link with the property made her sad.

Soon the track passed beside a paddock where sheep were running. The ewe suddenly made up her mind and, charging at a weak spot in the fence, she and the lamb shoved themselves onto their home territory. After that the wethers settled down.

The flock was quite large now and the woman judged that she had gathered up most of the sheep. She had earlier lost four along a cutting and would have to look for them another day. There was only one place now where she might have trouble, a creek crossing where the track widened on a corner. Dead gum trees had fallen on either side of the swampy ford, making a kind of race. If the sheep bunched up and ran together through this, without spreading out amongst the saplings on the bank, it would be easy enough. She must use patience.

As they reached the creek the mob held together well, but at the sight of the water they stopped nervously. She watched from behind a tree. One wether took a hesitating step, another followed. Again they stopped. She risked showing herself and, circling behind them, called like a barking dog and clapped her hands sharply.

The sudden disturbance was enough, and bravely the mob dashed through the water and tore up the hill on the far side while the woman scrambled up the steep banks of the creek. Running again, she managed to wheel them through the gate, left open in readiness, and into her own paddock. They careered about with crazy exuberance, some leaping and jumping high in nervous excitement. Inside they sobered at once and, beginning quietly to crop the good green clover, they slowly spread across the hillside.

Panting, she triumphantly shut the cocky gate behind them, twisting the iron bar into place and securing it with a ring of wire. She sat down on a boulder to rest. She was a tall, slender woman with an unconventional style and elegance about her, which impressed itself on all she did. Clad as she was at that moment in her customary work clothes, a man's shirt, old jeans and gumboots, she might have been outfitted by the best tailor and bespoke bootmaker. Her straight hair hung to her shoulders, neither grey nor blonde, and her lightly browned skin gave no indication of her age, though she had three grown children, two sons who lived in the city and a married daughter two states away. Her eyes held a look of considering appraisal, which might have seemed cold, but when she smiled they crinkled into kindness and lively warmth. Her thoughts turned to her husband and she addressed him in her mind, as she so often did.

"You would have been pleased with that. I only missed a few, and I'll get them tomorrow."

She could hear his reply. "Just take it gently, old girl." But her husband was dead.

He had died very suddenly, more than a year ago now, and she had not even had a chance to say goodbye. He had called through the house to her one morning:

"I'm taking the ute to pick up some sheep nuts. Anything you want?"

She was dressmaking and had not troubled to move, simply calling back, "No thanks, I've got everything. See you at lunch."

A passing motorist had found the ute smashed into a red

gum beside the main road, sheep nuts scattered like pebbles across the bitumen, and blood on the windscreen. Later the doctor said he must have had a heart attack before the car ran off the road. One of her sons chanced to be at home that day and persuaded her not to see the body. At the time she thought this right, but later regretted that she had not done so. However terrible, it would have been one last thing they would have shared.

Since then, he had occupied her thoughts constantly. Her mind was obsessed with his unseen presence. There was no room now for the refreshment of new ideas, and she grew weary and bone-thin as she talked to him silently. Yet, sitting on the boulder in the clear autumn sun, she suddenly realised that for the whole time that she had been mustering the sheep, she had thought only of her task. Briefly, she had been returned to herself and was at peace. Perhaps she was beginning to recover.

With thc hclp of a workman she was managing the property herself. Her two sons had begged her to come and live with them in the city, but she had refused. This was her home and she needed its reassurance now more than ever.

One great difficulty in her life, which she had noticed particularly this morning, was that her husband's sheep dog, Trixie, refused to work for her. When her master died, Trixie had pined for him pitifully, whining and searching all about the place, and the woman could hardly bear to see her distress. Her husband had always been adamant about working dogs living outside the house. They were not to be treated as pets. Trixie had her kennel under a pepper tree at the end of the yard and there she was chained when she was not with her master.

Her life had been a satisfying one; he always took her with him about the place and there was plenty for her to do. A black and white crossbreed, she had a feathery white tip to her tail and a smudge of white on her chest. Now she obstinately refused to obey commands from anyone. Neither the woman, her sons nor the workman could persuade her to work and, without work, she hardly had an existence. Whatever order they gave her, in whatever tone of voice, she simply lay flat on her belly and crawled supplicatingly towards them. Exercising the poor creature was a problem, but fortunately she would climb willingly enough into the station wagon and the woman would drive her a short distance every evening and make her run home behind the car. It was an extra burden which the woman had discussed many times with her sons. No one could bring themselves to have the bitch put down, though it almost seemed the kindest thing to do. This morning the woman had badly needed a good dog to help her.

She looked back across her neighbour's land. He had quarrelled with her shortly after her husband's death over a question of water rights, and she had not spoken to him since. She stood up and walked to the utility parked behind a clump of banksias.

The next day was benignly sunny and she was determined to find her missing wethers. She knew that there was a waterhole somewhere in the centre of the forest and thought that they might have camped nearby. She followed the course of the creek, barely a trickle and so narrow that wiry grasses and rushes almost covered it, which made a way for her through the forest. Huge toadstools, domed and shining damp brown, pushed aside their covering of pine needles. The warmth drew out the scent of pine whenever she brushed against a tree. Clusters of orange fungus scalloped the feet of occasional gum trees. Amongst the trees it was still and silent; no birds sang in the quiet gloom but sometimes overhead the wind ran across the tree tops with a sound like an approaching train.

The creek ended abruptly and she stepped from a tangle of scrub to find herself on the very edge of the waterhole. Partly natural, partly man-made long before the forest was planted, it was about nine metres long and almost square, the sides straight as those of a bath and decorated with ferns. It was entirely enclosed by trees, young pines as erect and orderly as rows of cadets and, at one end, a grove of gum saplings, feathery grey in the autumn sun. The still brown water was clear, unstained by mud and unpolluted by reeds; its polished steel surface reflected the trees above it in exact detail. There were no sheep in sight, but so great was the beauty of the scene that she was compelled to stand for several minutes to absorb it all.

It was hot in this sheltered place, and the need to pay homage to such a morning came upon her, to plunge into the pure dark water. Quickly she stripped off her clothes and stood naked on the fine grass. As she looked down into the water below her, a glimmering of intense happiness came to her, like a scent tantalising the nostrils with a faint memory. The balmy air caressed her body in a way that no man had done for so long and aroused desires in her that she thought she had put aside. She ran delicate fingers around her breasts, across her belly and down her flanks. Then she dived into the water.

Across the pool, hidden by a tree, stood a tall man watching her. His work shirt was as blue as the shadows and his piercing eyes blue like his shirt. His skin, tanned by outdoor work, had something of the texture of pine bark. He had been standing there when she emerged from the trees, but had not thought to disclose his presence. When she began to undress this had seemed as natural as the day. She embodied the spirit of the place. So he watched gravely as she dropped her clothes to the ground and stood up straight. He saw that her nipples were as pink as the new tips on the end of the pine branches pointing to the sky. He had no wish to disturb her and when she entered the water he quickly turned and strode silently away through the trees.

The next time he saw her she was decorously clad and in a much more prosaic situation. It was at the saleyards in the local town and she was standing diagonally opposite him across a milling sea of woolly backs. Wearing a swinging skirt as russet as the pine needles on the forest floor and a little jacket to match over a high necked white jumper, her slender legs looked even longer in her high, tan boots. He noticed how well-polished they were, which pleased him, and he glanced down at his own elastic sides, gleaming as usual beneath his immaculate moleskins. He stared openly, taking in every detail about her. Though they had never exchanged a word, she had a fresh quality which drew him to her at once. She moved in a way that set her aside from those around her.

It was a disagreeable day. A gritty wind blew dirt in his eyes, and farmers pulled their felt hats lower on their foreheads, muttering cautious asides to one another. Heavy clouds spat a prickle of rain over the yards. The auctioneer moved quickly from one pen to the next, his voice the only clear sound above the bleating of the uneasy sheep. "Done, done, all done," and a clap of the hands.

After a long drought there had been good rains; feed was plentiful and both the man and the woman were buying lambs to fatten and increase their depleted flocks. So they were interested in the same lots and there was a rivalry between them.

When all was over he saw her arranging to have her lambs trucked to her property and he determined to speak to her. He stepped beside her and made a kind of salute.

"I don't know if you remember me, but we used to know each other years ago when we were at school."

She paused, aloof, taking in his looks and his manner of speech. Then she flared into friendliness and held out her hand.

"Of course I remember you. Have you come to live at Glenbarr?" Then she caught herself. "I'm sorry — I'm afraid your brother and I had certain difficulties. We haven't spoken for some time."

"Yes, I know, and it's a pity — I hope we can change that. As it happens, he's had to go and live in the city because of his arthritis. I think the constant pain sometimes made things hard for him. I'm running the place now. It's many years since I've been in this part of the world — I've been in New Guinea. But when you grow up on a place you never lose the feel of it and I'm gradually finding my way about. I'd be glad of advice from you."

She was appeased, not being one to bear grudges, and they shook hands. He noticed what a hard little grip she had.

"Will you have a cup of coffee with me?" he asked her.

"I'd rather have a beer," she said. "The pub's noisy, but the coffee shop is a desert."

He liked that and they found a table where they could talk, giving each other details of their lives. He had never married, having had little opportunity to meet the kind of woman who would want to share his life in the wild New Guinea highlands, and he had been so busy with his administrative work that he scarcely noticed his loneliness. Though the new government had valued his knowledge so highly that they had kept him on for some years, his term had finally ended recently, just when it was opportune for him to return to Glenbarr.

She mentioned again her unfortunate arguments with his brother, hoping to discuss the matter reasonably, but the rivalry that had been sparked off over the lambs, a deal in which she had done rather better than he, still held and there was a slight tension between them yet.

"I'm sure my brother didn't mean to be as difficult as you think," the man said stiffly, family feelings uppermost. He regretted his words at once, for he knew that justice was on her side, and the last thing he wanted to do was to quarrel with her.

"I think that under the circumstances he might have been more agreeable." She, too, could be stiff.

Suddenly he laughed and said forthrightly: "You mean you want to be treated as a man because you are doing man's job, but you want special consideration because you're a woman?"

She flung up her chin and looked furiously into his eyes, but there was something gentle in his face which tempered his rude words. She capitulated.

"Yes, I believe that's exactly it."

"Well, now we're both being honest."

No one had been brave enough to use this tone to her for a long time and she found it stimulating. They parted in a friendly way, though each had a sense that they were sparring for position.

A few days later she walked into her office to find the canvas mailbag lying on her desk and, sorting her letters, found that one directed to Glenbarr had been included by mistake. It would be pleasant, she thought, and would do away with the last of the neighbourly ill-feeling if she took the letter to the man herself. She unchained Trixie and coaxed her into the back of the station wagon. It would be an outing for her and she could run a few kilometres on the way back. Trixie was beginning to be more enthusiastic about her evening run, though she still cringed and nothing would persuade her to work. Now she pressed her nose to the half-open window, streaked with the smears from previous outings, and her far-seeing eyes took in all the passing countryside. She understood the meaning of the smells which came to her through the window.

They pulled up at the back gate beside the homestead. The woman was a stranger here now, where once she had known the house so well. At the back door she knocked and knocked again, but there was no answer. Clearly the man was not in from the paddocks yet, and she decided to leave the letter on the kitchen table. The hall was cluttered with boots and waterproofs, as it always had been, and there was a smell of rubber and disinfectant which she well remembered. She stepped into the kitchen and noticed that the dresser still held the rose-patterned cups and plates that had always been there. She laid the letter on the scrubbed table and was about to return to the car when there was a sudden fury of barking dogs outside the window. Two sheep dogs flew round the corner of the house and headed straight towards the station wagon whence Trixie screamed at them through the window. The woman was hurrying outside to quiet her when, to her dismay, she saw that the window was half down and Trixie was scrabbling through it, ready for a fight.

The man appeared and ran, yelling, after his dogs, but there was no stopping them now. Snapping, shrieking, rolling and tearing — the fight was in full swing. He grabbed a hose and turned it on the animals, which finally separated them. Catching Trixie by the fur on her back, he flung her into the car, and his own dogs slunk away. There was a great deal of foaming slobber and some blood, but none of the dogs was seriously hurt, it seemed. The man was in a raging temper.

"Who the bloody hell brought that bitch onto the place?" he shouted at the top of his voice. "They ought to have more sense."

The woman, caught at a double disadvantage, walked out the door.

"I'm afraid it was my fault," she said haughtily, angry that she seemed to be in the wrong. "I came with a letter for you and forgot to wind up the car window. I'm sorry if your dogs are hurt."

Her tone implied that they thoroughly deserved to be bitten for their churlishness. The two of them stood glaring at each other, the man exposed by his rudeness as he did not want to be. He began to say something but, as he hesitated, she jumped into the car and drove away before he could speak.

She was quickly offended these days and her own hot temper had boiled over in a flash. She was still shaking when she stopped to let Trixie have her run and to examine her wounds. There appeared to be nothing disastrous: a torn ear and one tooth mark on her neck which went deep and would need treatment when they reached home, but that was all. She began to recover herself and thought ruefully of the object of her visit and how unsuccessful it had been. It was largely her fault, though she was hardly prepared to admit that, even to herself. She longed for her husband to sympathise with her. He would always loyally take her side, but she did wonder after a while if she might not hear his familiar, "Take it gently, old girl."

He had said it to her so often.

As she drove away the man stared after her, amazed that she was gone so quickly. The sentence on his tongue disappeared into midair. Now he was not even certain whether he had intented to be conciliatory or not. He was still angry, angry with himself for his violent reaction to the dog fight, angry with the woman for putting him in an unfavourable position, leaving him standing foolishly and mouthing words to which no one was listening.

As the days went by he thought what an absurd episode it had been and was almost ready to tell the story against himself. In spite of himself he knew there was a strange bond between them, a sense of some particular feeling. He did not see her again for some weeks, and then it was only in the distance as she carried a box of fruit from the greengrocer's in the town one day. She seemed to stand out from her surroundings as if she were the only person in focus in a blurred photograph. His eyes could hardly leave her as he chatted with a group of men by the Post Office and he longed for her to stop there so he could speak to her. But she had already collected her mail and drove away. He thought wryly that he was beginning to grow familiar with the sight of her station wagon disappearing into the distance.

He gossiped about her as discreetly as possible in the grocery store and the newsagent's and discovered that she was much liked in the town; she took her part in local affairs and was on the board of the hospital. She was respected for her decision to stay on her property, though there were some who doubted whether it would not prove too difficult an undertaking for her. So he filled in a picture of her character without her having any idea that he thought about her at all.

He was enjoying his new life, being used to living alone. Though in New Guinea he had had a boy who cooked his meals, he found it pleasant in the evenings to prepare his own dinner and discovered a new interest in cooking exotic dishes. He planted a vegetable garden and, when that was successful, began work on a herbaceous border round the lawn in front of the house. He happily spent his time striking cuttings and setting out plants from friends' gardens. His other pleasure was his flute, which had been his companion since boyhood and which he usually played each evening for an hour. With his interest in music went an ability in mathematics, and he started putting the station books and records in order. The station prospered with his attention.

The woman struggled through the winter days as best she could. This was the second winter since her husband's death, but the first had been so taken up with practical arrangements and the kind attention of friends that she could hardly remember how it had passed. Now it was much more difficult; her pain was not cushioned by these activities, nor numbed by exceptional circumstances. Her mind was still tormented with the memories of her husband and his presence in absence which dominated her life. Surprisingly, the nights were not as difficult as she had expected. Somehow she managed to sleep. It was the early mornings which she found hardest to bear. As she filled the kettle to make her breakfast coffee and knew she had another whole day before her, she almost despaired of being able to creep through the hours. To have reached midday was already an achievement. There was only half the day left and, as evening drew in, there was little endurance still needed. The hours of respite were at hand.

Trixie nearly died in the first cold weeks. The bite on her neck turned septic and, growling and snapping whenever her mistress touched the wound, she had to be muzzled for dressings. At first it seemed that she would not survive, but the woman nursed her tenaciously, determined that she would live. When at last the danger was over and Trixie was lying feebly in the sun by her kennel, she felt a devotion to the dog in a way that she had never done before.

She often thought of her neighbour through this time, though not resentfully. She was sufficiently fair-minded to know that she could not blame him. There was no feud between them, and nor was there friendship, yet she, too, was conscious that there was some thread pulling them together. She was curious about him but determined, in her obstinate way, that no conciliatory move would come from her.

She brought home a black and white kitten for company. It sat on the arm of her chair as she read or sewed, sometimes dabbing a cold little paw at her needle. The relentless talking continued in her head, and she knew that she sometimes spoke aloud because the kitten would prick its ears forward and open its eyes round and wide, green as little apples.

Bad weather did not trouble her. Storms suited her mood

and brought her out of herself. She preferred to be outside in the wind and the rain. It was the clear shining days following the storms that awoke in her involuntary responses of joy and delight which, for their fulfilment, craved the companionship of someone beloved. Her sons were thoughtful and visited her whenever possible and her friends were affectionate, but there was still a deep emptiness which had to be faced alone.

Then one day something happened which she thought of afterwards as a miracle, though at the time it seemed a kind of joke and surely, she thought, miracles were serious matters. One soft, damp morning as she stood in her garden, she noticed that the daffodils were already pushing their way indomitably through the soil, so far had the season advanced. She remembered the place where she had dug up the bulbs. Some miles away at the end of the run stood the ruins of a tumbledown stone cottage, with only the chimney and the arched bread oven still intact, and with the remains of a crumbling wall holding a finely carved architrave above an empty doorway. The outlines of the garden could still be seen clearly — an almond tree at the gate, a hedge of olive trees on one side and a twisted fig tree. She and wanted to dig up some bulbs she had marked the previous year and had known that this month one bed would be full of curly-petalled scarlet and pink nerines for her to pick.

Like most farmers her husband disliked eating his meals out of doors, but one halcyon day she persuaded him to come with her, packing his favourite foods in the picnic basket: a jar of her own special dill pickles, the orange cake he always liked. He was amused and touched by these attentions and they enjoyed themselves enormously. When she told him a funny anecdote about a friend, his laugh, one of the things she loved best about him, rang out as freely as a child's. They sat in the shade of a gum tree and she threaded a chain of late dandelion heads. He leapt to his feet and, with his pocket knife, marked the silvery trunk above them.

"There, I've always wanted to do that! I was never allowed when I was a boy."

"What have you done? Did you carve our initials?"

She jumped up to look. About five centimetres high, they were cut into the tree.

"Aren't you ashamed?" she teased him. "At your age."

"Well, they're so tiny no one will ever notice them except for you and me." And they kissed.

That afternoon she had arrived home with her bulbs and her bunch of nerines and then remembered, too late, that she had left her secateurs on the old hearth. He died soon afterwards and she had carefully avoided the place ever since. Now, as she looked at the spikes of green standing up in the earth, she thought it ridiculous that she should leave a perfectly good pair of secateurs there. She would go at once and fetch them. Trixie, convalescent, would come with her.

Near the cottage, wattles were already flowering, pungent and full of tinkling birds. She quickly found her secateurs, just where she had left them; they were rusty now, but that could be cured. Trixie nosed for lizards and fieldmice under an old wooden beam. The woman wandered about the garden and found jonquils flowering in one corner, their scent blowing sweetly towards her. The atmosphere of the place was not distressing; it was soothing and healing, and she wished she had gone there sooner. So softened was her mood that her eyes filled with tears, though she seldom cried. She was not a weeper and was denied this comfort. She found herself under the gum tree where they had picnicked and, putting out her hand to stroke it, looked up at the curving white trunk.

There above her, orange-red and resinous against the powdery whiteness of the trunk, stood the initials which her husband had carved, eighteen centimetres high now and, between them, the shape of a heart, more vivid than if he had painted it. She had not even noticed the heart before. It was as though he had sent her a direct message. As she gasped, almost cried out, she clearly heard his laugh behind her, just as she had heard it so often and particularly on the day of their picnic.

"Take it gently, old girl," she heard him say, and she swung round to speak to him.

There was no one there but Trixie, who put up her head and gave a great flurry of barks.

In that moment something in her was released; her torture was over. Her grief went with her always, but she found consolation in her mourning.

Some weeks later there came one of those days when summer seems to have stepped into the middle of winter and briefly to hold sway. The woman could not help being glad when she saw the blossom trees burgeoning under the cobalt sky. In this mood she impulsively decided that it was time to make peace with her neighbour, that their foolish differences must be resolved. Apologies did not come easily to her; they were contrary to her nature, but she felt she must make a great effort to put aside any pettiness. One of them had to take the first step and perhaps it must be she.

She chose midday to make her visit, thinking to find him home for his lunch, and she was right. He was planting seedlings when he heard her step and, looking up, saw her walking towards him. It was as though he had known she was coming and he stood up, wiping his hands on his trousers.

They shook hands, smiling at each other.

"I'm so sorry," she began.

"Whatever for, I'm sorry too."

And that was the last reference to the incident.

"Do you mind if I finish putting in these seedings — they'll get dry if I leave them."

"What are they?"

"Pansies. I love the colours."

"I see you've got carrots coming through. Do you plant them with radishes?"

"No — is that a good idea?"

So they exchanged gardening lore and he showed her his herbaceous border which she admired, promising to bring him some blue penstemons from her own garden. Under a quince tree they sat and drank a bottle of white wine and talked, watching the honey-eaters sipping from a fuchsia bush.

"I must go now," she said, standing up resolutely.

"Will you come again?"

"Yes."

"Will you marry me?"

Their conversation had been so light that he surprised even himself with his question, unpremeditated and expressed in a tone of formality. She replied, equally courteously, as if this were a perfectly ordinary enquiry.

"I can't. You see, I'm married already."

Then, as if they more deeply understood what each had said, she made a little helpless gesture towards him and walked quickly away, leaving him standing looking after her.

The next day she was in a turmoil, hardly able to understand her own tumultuous thoughts, expecting he would come and hoping he would not. She avoided leaving the house and looked for him a hundred times. In the late afternoon she decided to collect the mail in the town, so that she nearly missed his visit when he did come, driving up just as he was about to go away.

They walked towards each other, her hair blowing delicately around her face, his eyes more blue than ever in the sunset glow.

"I meant it," he said. "Will you marry me?"

She did not touch him and he could see that she was untouchable, holding herself away from him, alone, straight and slim.

"I will, if you can make Trixie work for you," she replied.

He was angry, insulted; she was mocking him, he thought. He paused, choked by the words in his throat, and looked silently at her. She stared straight back, challenging him. He understood. If she had been his mistress in times gone by, she might have laid such a task upon him. But his anger held.

"I will work Trixie," he said. "I'll bring your sheep back to you, with her help — there are more in the forest than you thought. Tomorrow morning."

So they parted and, the die being cast, each slept dreamlessly that night.

Not long after first light she was waiting for him at her paddock gate. A fog lay among the pine trees and there seemed to be fire under the earth as swirls of mist rose like smoke from the ground. A rosy light behind the fog and glimpses of blue high above meant that the sun would shine later, but now the white obscurity would make the business of rounding up sheep more difficult.

Trixie lay at her feet and, her head sunk on her paws, seemed to be sulking. Only her eyebrows flickered as she moved her eyes quickly from side to side, observing the morning. She clearly understood that this was an unusual day, while her mistress nervously stamped her feet to keep them warm and rubbed her gloved hands together.

Suddenly the man came out of the fog, riding on a bay mare, his brown waterproof jacket glistening with moisture.

Horse and rider were all of a colour and seemed immensely tall, magnified by the fog. The horse was fresh and nervous, but he handled her easily.

Their greeting was short, almost as though they had not parted.

"Trixie has never worked with a horse," she said hesitantly, almost ready to concede a point. "She's used to a motorbike or working on foot."

The horse tossed her head and he walked her in a tight circle, soothing her with quiet words.

"Then she's going to learn something new now," he replied briefly, and the woman knew that there would be no concessions today.

"The sheep are camping on the next ridge. If you leave the gate open and stand behind the banksias, you can count them as they come through," he said calmly.

Their eyes met but, though he was so high above her, there was such spirit in her gaze that she was not dwarfed by him.

"You had better go now," she said.

Trixie watched them, her chin on the ground, her tail motionless.

He turned his horse and, as he rode away into the fog, looked over his shoulder and gave a long piercing whistle.

Trixie jerked up her head, ears cocked, incredulous. There was something in this man's manner which forced her to respond. Slowly her tail moved, sweeping from side to side. It was as if she had been waiting to hear a certain note, without which she had had no power to act. He whistled again and she stood up, still uncertain, but feeling the compulsion to work coming upon her. She must play her rightful part; this was what her life was meant for.

"Heel, Trixie," he called, and she accepted him at last. She tore away after him. A great lump rose in the woman's throat.

She stood where she was as he disappeared from sight. The fog was lifting and, after a time, she could hear him calling in the distance. His commands became clearer as he approached and she heard the footfalls and bleating of the sheep.

"Back, back, get away back, Trixie. Stay. Stay. Over there."

Trixie rushed out of the trees and, galloping along the track, turned the sheep through the gate with all her old skill.

The woman counted ten of them as they went by and then closed the gate on them. Standing there, she knew that if this was a contest, she willingly conceded him the winner and she waited for him, as elated as if she had triumphed.

The man rode up. The sun, breaking through the mist, lit up his bare head. Trixie, panting, tongue lolling, her tense joyousness an extraordinary contrast to her previous behaviour, danced at the horse's feet.

"There are your sheep," he said almost roughly. "I shall take Trixie with me." Wheeling his horse, he rode away, Trixie trotting at his heels without looking back to where her mistress stood alone and bewildered, uncertain as to how her life had changed.

For two days there was no word from him. She did not know what she had expected, but not complete silence. Perhaps he had changed his mind; perhaps he thought she had changed her own. She wondered if he were trying to humble her, but could not believe he had such a streak of cruelty in his make-up. She was puzzled and apprehensive, doubting and hoping all at once. At one moment she decided to go away to the city, but almost at the same moment decided to remain home.

On the third day the sun shone gloriously and increased her restlessness. She went about the house and yard, picked a few flowers, was unable to settle to anything for long. At midday a lad who did odd jobs in the area delivered a letter to her, a letter in a big solid blue envelope.

Will you meet me by the pool in the forest? I will wait there for you, was the message.

Heart pounding, knees trembling, she made her way through the trees, the sun hot on her face. Halfway there she wondered if perhaps she should have changed out of her old working clothes; she must look a mess. She nearly ran back, but it was too late; he would hear her and think she was running away from him. She saw Trixie before she saw him. The dog came running to meet her, plumed tail waving joyfully, and led her to where the man was standing.

The still water reflected the two figures as they held out their arms to each other, clasped and embraced. Trixie sank silently to the ground. Her eyebrows twitched as she gazed up at them.